Reading Buddies

Penny Pentley

FIVE CENTS PUBLISHING

To my best teacher friend,
Thanks for helping me keep my sanity in those first years of teaching
(and for inspiring parts of this story).

CHAPTER 1

The New Job

Jesus Christ, how did I end up here? Wait. I should stop using the term "Jesus Christ." Can I get fired for that?

I pull the contract—not contract, *covenant*—out from the protective sleeve and flip to the final page. "All Catholic school employees are expected to publicly model the traditions and practices of the Roman Catholic Church. This covenant may be terminated if the teacher's lifestyle or conduct is found to go against Catholic moral teaching and values." I wonder if using the Lord's name in vain is considered conduct that goes against moral teaching...

My boyfriend, Charlie, is putting the finishing touches on our coffees. One sugar and cream for him, two teaspoons of Ovaltine and a splash of milk for me. Don't judge me. It has vitamins. He rests his chin on my shoulder as he sets down my oversized Disney mug. "What are you worrying about now?"

I shrug him off. "I just know I'm going to mess this up. I'm going to do or say the wrong thing and then, *boom*. Fired."

"And then you can just sub again. We will be no worse off than we were last school year." He wanders over to his laptop on the other side of our living space and parks himself there. He will probably not move until I return this afternoon. "It is just orientation, anyway. Just play the good Catholic girl from eight to three and then you can be your normal heathen-y self when you get home."

I sigh at the paper before tucking it back into its proper place. Last year I subbed nearly every day. I made good money, too. The public schools were so desperate for subs, there was almost always somewhere to go. There was even bonus money on the high-demand days that surrounded long weekends and holiday breaks. The problem with that was hardly ever knowing where I was going from day to day. I'd never see the same kids for more than a week at a time—and those full weeks were only if the teacher planned to be gone ahead of time. Most of the time, I would wake up at five in the morning to see which schools needed someone, then take whichever job was closest to home or my favorite lunch spots. Then I spend half an hour reading over the sub notes (if there even are any) and throw myself into the chaos of an elementary classroom without their captain.

Some days were great. Everything was organized, the kids had solid routines that could be used by visiting teachers, and there was a clear plan of what I was expected to do for the day. Some days were complete shit. I won't go into detail, but there was more than one teacher I had on my "do not take jobs for" list.

Having *my own* class would be fantastic. Not only would I be able to see the same kids every day, watch them grow and learn, but I could help develop the procedures and routines. I could get to know what makes them tick—and I sure as hell would make sure to put in sub plans "watch out for this kid because he likes to kick." I rubbed the part of my calf where the epic bruise had been. It was purple for an entire month.

My eyes are drawn to the clock and I jolt upright, delicately taking one last pull of my coffee before grabbing my bag from the chair next to me, kissing Charlie on the cheek, and heading out the front door. I can't help but glance at his laptop. *Page seven? Wasn't he on page seven last week?* It is going to be hard for him to make it as an author if he isn't *writing* anything. *Maybe he will make more progress with me out of the house again.*

I jump in the beater car we share and the radio blasts the classic rock station that Charlie likes. I turn the knob until it hits the Top 40 channel I prefer. We had an aux cord that went to the tape player at some point, but then the tape player broke. Now we are a radio couple.

I drive by two public schools on the way. Both were supposed to have job openings this year. I made sure to stay up to date with the rumor mills at each of them. I even subbed for two of the teachers who were retiring this year. Fortunately and unfortunately, the teachers' unions negotiated higher salaries, which meant they had to merge classes to keep on budget. As teachers left, they just shifted the students that were supposed to be theirs into the other classes at that grade level. The few jobs that opened were filled by people with decades of experience. I couldn't even get an interview.

I *was* able to manage an interview for the local Catholic school, though. I'd gone to Catholic school growing up, a nice little K-8 just like this one, but after I left for high school, I never stepped foot in a church again, save for the occasional wedding or funeral. After doing a quick refresher on my catechism and locating my baptism and confirmation certificates, I rocked the interview with the principal and a few veteran teachers. While looking over my resume, one teacher commented that her year of subbing prepared her for classroom management better than her teacher training program had, which gave me the idea she was really pulling for me. Religion was barely touched on.

Unfortunately, neither was the pay. You know those unions the public schools have here? Yeah, parochial schools don't get those, and as a result, I will make $15,000 less than I would at one of those schools I just drove by. All while keeping my personal life under serious lock and key.

The school is a massive brick rectangle on a side street I'd driven by hundreds of times since I moved out here, but never went down until the day of my interview. I park and follow a woman with a long, blonde ponytail, her arms full of cloth, up the stairs to the front door. I weasel my way in front of her to hold open the door.

"Thanks!" she says as she peeks her head out from around a few bolts. I recognize her as one of the teachers who helped interview me.

"You're welcome. Finch, right?" I ask, pushing myself against the door so she could go by.

"Yep. I'm Amanda, but you can just call me Miss Finch if you want to for now." She took the stairs slowly, readjusting her arms to not lose anything. "It's easier to use teacher names first so you know what the kids call us. Nothing more awkward than asking a student to give a message to Amanda and them having no idea who you're talking about."

"Let me help you with those." I reach out, hovering under a precariously placed bolt of bright blue fabric.

"Yeah, if you can just take that one there, I think I can handle the rest."

We manage to finagle the one bolt out without losing the others. "I'll walk you to your room. What's with the fabric, anyway? Are the kids making their own uniforms?" We walk down the wide hallway, long fluorescent bulbs lighting our way, reflecting off a freshly waxed floor. This would be the shiniest I would ever see it.

"If you make a bulletin board with fabric, they last *so much* longer. It costs more, but they don't fade or tear like butcher paper. I'm four years in and tired of having to re-do the bulletin board backgrounds annually." She stops outside a closed door and sighs. "My keys are in my purse. Do you mind?" She turns around so her purse is directly in front of me. "Just find the pink lanyard and pull."

I eye her, waiting to see if she changes her mind about a stranger going through her purse, but when she shakes her elbow, moving the bag, I unzip it and find the keys tucked in next to a cell phone and a few tampons.

"It's the big one. Not the round big one, but the more jagged big one."

The two largest keys are just as she described—I drop the one with the smooth grip and use the other one, opening the door to the smell of stale classroom. All the walls are bare and the only light is coming in from the tall windows.

Amanda enters and drops the bolts unceremoniously on the ground. "Don't you just love the blank slate of a new year?"

Her energy hits me like a wave. I had been so unsure how to feel walking into this, and my brain decided to stick with nervousness, but I am about to start my first year as a classroom teacher. I would get time today to set up my classroom, write my students' names on the nametags I bought at the dollar store, decide what I am going to do for the first day of school, and pave the way for all the days after. For the first time since looking at that covenant, I am *excited*.

"You better get to the break room before all the good breakfast treats are gone. Jim—Mr. Gallagher—will take any maple bars that aren't claimed by the time the meeting starts. I have no idea how the man stays so fit."

"I'm alright, I had a coffee before I—"

"Don't let Mrs. Smith hear you say that," Amanda scolds. "She works very hard on the breakfast spreads."

I remember Mrs. Smith, the secretary, from my interview. She was a little matter-of-fact, working on multiple things when I came into the office. I didn't get a smile when I greeted her or told her why I was there. I understood, though. When you're dealing with every problem in the school at once for nine months out of the year, you don't have time to paste a smile on your face. Many school secretaries I've met are the same way. Once a certain student comes through the door, though, they tend to light up.

I know that I want to be on Mrs. Smith's good side. While she's dealing with a hundred fires at once, you want your fire to be toward the top of the list of ones being put out. Another helpful thing I've learned in my days of subbing. "I'll head up and eat something, then. Are you coming?"

Amanda admires the fabric she unrolled, then looks to the board she wants to cover, and back. "I guess it's not going anywhere, unlike those doughnuts."

One more flight of stairs and we are on the top floor. On the left is the library, where people are sitting at tables with plates of food and disposable cups of coffee. On the right, people are filing in and out of a small, narrow room. When we finally push our way in, the tables down the center of the room are filled with doughnuts, a large bowl of fruit, bagels, cream cheese and jam, and three containers of coffee with all the fixings. The toaster in the kitchenette is working overtime, and the smell of slightly burned carbs fills the room in the best way possible.

I grab a plate and reach for a doughnut, noticing a man in a long-sleeve button-up shirt eyeing me as I do so. I shift my hand away from the two remaining maple bars and grab a plain glazed ring. The remaining space gets filled with fruit. I pass by the coffee but see there are hot cocoa packets next to the sugars, so I make a plan to come back during a break.

Amanda leads me to a table in the library where the other teacher who interviewed me is already sitting. I want to say her name has something to do with the rosary. Her plate is empty, but she is sipping on her coffee as her eyes betray a smile when she sees Amanda approach.

"You can't have news already," Amanda whispers as she sits down across from her.

"Nothing concrete yet, but I think Cheryl is pregnant."

Amanda turns around for a few seconds and stares directly at another teacher wearing a tunic and leggings. "There is no way. She is drinking coffee."

"She has been nursing this one cup since I got here. Mrs. Smith had the dream," she says, as if that was the end of the conversation. She looks at me and smiles. "I'm glad Mark chose you. I think we all felt like you'd be a good fit. Mrs. Monroe, right?"

I nod, correcting, "*Miss* Monroe. Danielle. I'm so sorry I can't remember your name right now."

"That is quite alright. You probably had loads of interviews and met so many people this summer. I didn't expect you to remember. I'm Alice, Mrs. del Rosario to the kids. I teach Kindergarten." Alice turns back to look the possibly-pregnant teacher up and down. "She never wears leggings. She only ever wears jeans on in-service days. I'm telling you, she's pregnant."

Amanda bites a raspberry off her fork, then uses it to point at Alice. "Fine. I bet you one pack of whiteboard markers that she is *not* pregnant."

Alice raises her eyebrows. "It better be the 16-count with all the pretty colors."

"Mmm. I love that teal on a nice, clean whiteboard."

Their negotiation is interrupted by the principal standing, going back to his coffee for one last sip before starting the meeting. Principal Mark is a balding man with a bit of a dad bod; he kind of reminds me of my dad. When he opens with a dad joke, it solidifies the likeness. "Good morning, everyone! I hope you had a wonderful summer break. Besides a two-week vacation with the family, I spent most of the summer doing what your students do all year—trying to solve teachers' problems."

He gets no actual laughs, but the sound of air being forced through nostrils can be heard throughout the room. He starts the meeting with a prayer, asking for intentions from the teachers.

When Cheryl speaks up, asking for a safe and healthy pregnancy, a few teachers give polite congratulations while Alice sneakily nudges Amanda. Other teachers pray for sick parents, for a brother in trouble with the law, for last year's eighth graders in their first year of high school, and for a great school year. We end with the Lord's

Prayer, which I still mostly have memorized, though I mumble my way through it just in case something's changed in the past decade.

Mark moves in front of the whiteboard, writing down the order of events for the morning. The first says "Icebreaker." I do everything in my power not to groan. I hate icebreakers. I always have. I never know what to say, and if I don't go first, I end up shaking from the building nerves from waiting.

"I actually didn't plan which icebreaker to do." Mark shrugs as he sets down his marker. "If any of you have suggestions, let's hear them."

The teachers look side to side, waiting for someone to suggest something. My nerves are already building and, if we don't get this started soon, I'm going to be trembling like a brick wall in an earthquake. Before I fully think it through, my hand shoots up. "Never have I ever?" My face freezes. Did I just suggest a game I learned as a drinking game in a frat basement?

Amanda claps her hands together. "Yes! Never have I ever!" She holds both her hands up in front of her, fingers spread. Alice and a few of the other teachers do the same.

Mrs. Smith is standing, leaning against the door frame, reading glasses pushed up onto her head, indicating that something might pull her away at any minute. "Could you explain how to play, for us... older folks?"

I let out a nervous laugh. "Yeah, uh..." I hold up my fingers, too. "Each person says something they have never done, and if you *have* done it, you put one of your fingers down. So, if I were to start, I would say: never have I ever had my own class. So if you *have* had your own class, you put one of your fingers down."

Most people put a finger down. I see maybe six or seven who don't, including Mrs. Smith, a woman in a paint-spattered apron (the art teacher, most likely), a man wearing basketball shorts (PE, perhaps?), and a few others.

Amanda speaks next. "Never have I ever been on the roof of this building." A surprising number of fingers go down. I realize I will need to ask about this later.

Alice takes her turn. "Never have I ever used the basement restrooms." Almost everyone puts a finger down.

We move around the room, each person giving me a little more insight into the overall vibe of the school and its staff.

Then we come to a tall gentleman in jeans and an unbuttoned shirt over a graphic tee. He, like me, still has all his fingers up. He scans the room, then looks directly at me with warm, brown eyes. In the back of my mind, I register that he is pretty cute. "Never have I ever worked at a Catholic school." He and I are the only ones who keep our fingers up.

A conspiratorial smile creeps onto his face as his eyebrows raise and it seems to take my breath away. I break eye contact, trying to stop myself from blushing. But why am I blushing? Probably just the thought of being found out as a new teacher.

CHAPTER 2

The New Class

After a morning of going over schedules, signing up for recess duties, and a short scripture reflection from the parish priest, it is finally time for lunch. Mrs. Smith *had* ducked out of the meeting, but not to do anything in the office. When we go into the break room, there are platters of sandwiches and veggie trays. I snag half a turkey and half a ham, as well as a handful of carrots before squeezing my way back out of the narrow room. I head downstairs to the office where I see Mrs. Smith nibbling at her own lunch with one hand while answering emails with the other.

"Hi, Mrs. Smith. Any chance I can get a key for my classroom?" I gesture behind me, as my door can be seen from the office window. This proximity will probably come in handy for bathroom breaks or emergencies.

She sets down her sandwich, brushing her fingertips on a cloth napkin resting on her lap. She grabs some keys from under her desk and opens a cabinet. She looks over her shoulder for a second before looking back. "Good timing, Mr. Johnson. Miss Monroe is here for her key, too."

I turn around to see the tall gentleman from this morning towering over me. He is at least a full head taller than I am. I finally get a good look at the shirt hiding under his button-up—it's a topographic map of a mountain.

"Mt. Hood?" I ask.

He looks down at his shirt, pulling it out to check. "Yeah. Good eye."

"You had to look to remember which mountain was on your shirt?"

"I have one of Mt. Jefferson, too. Couldn't remember which one I put on today."

"Have you climbed those two?"

He laughs, shaking his head. "No. I'm not sure I have the coordination for much more than hiking. I did study both of them in undergrad, though. Geology major. I thought I would go on to volcanology, but—" he shrugs "—the classroom called to me."

"Here you are," Mrs. Smith interrupts, holding out a key in each hand. "We don't have copies, so try not to lose those, or Mr. Williams will have to pick the lock to get you into your rooms."

I take the key, thanking her before I head across the hall to my door.

"Looks like I'll be on top of you this year," Mr. Johnson says as he leaves the office.

I pause, holding off on my response until I get some kind of context; though my mind has a specific picture already painted.

"The science room is one flight up."

I finish unlocking my door, giving a polite grin as I turn around. "In my last apartment, the upstairs neighbors were quite a nuisance. Hopefully you're not the same."

He traces an X over his heart. "I will be on my best behavior. No promises for the middle schoolers, though."

I sigh. "It's going to be loud, isn't it?"

He closes his eyes, nodding slowly.

I point to my door. "I'm going to go eat my lunch. Nice to meet you."

"Did we actually meet, though? I'm Adam."

"Danielle."

He gives a wave as he turns to go up the stairs. I watch him go for what I quickly realize is too long, then pop into my classroom to eat my lunch. The sandwiches are *delicious*, but I regret not grabbing something to drink. My water bottle is still in my car along with all my supplies, so when I finish my carrots, I head out to ferry boxes and bags inside.

On my final trip, I find Amanda waiting at my classroom door with some papers tucked under her arm. She opens it for me, since I was *determined* to make this the last load and my arms were overflowing with odds and ends. She walks in behind me, holding out one of the papers. "Class lists are in! You might get one or two added in the next two days, but this is the bulk of your first class."

I set everything I have on the back table. "How many?" I ask, a bit hesitantly. Some of the classrooms I subbed in ended up with 26 or 27 kids when the cap was supposed to be 25. I didn't even ask if this school capped the number of students allowed in a class.

Amanda squints at the paper. "Twenty-three. Not bad for first grade." She looks down the list. "Alice's class last year was pretty chill, and most of them stayed, so hopefully they'll be good for you, too."

I take two of the desks that are stacked along the wall and flip them right-side-up. "How many do you have?"

"Only eighteen, but it's never a good omen when you get a class that another teacher left the profession after having."

"Wow, were they really that bad?" I realize I should have asked in the interview *why* my predecessor left.

Amanda laughs. "No, the kids were fine. She got a job in travel. She gets to go all over the world to see if her company's guidebooks are still accurate."

I dig through some bags to find the name plates I bought the other week and a permanent marker.

Amanda hands me the class list and holds up her own pack of name plates. "Great minds." She sits at the second desk and sets out her supplies.

My hand shakes as I start to write the first name: Christine. When I finish, it looks *alright*. I set it aside to dry, and to possibly re-do should I have enough extras.

Amanda eyes it. "Not bad. Your teacher handwriting is already coming along."

"My mom used to make me rewrite my homework if it wasn't neat enough. I think of her every time I am complimented on my handwriting." I start on the next name. Carter. It looks nearly perfect, so it makes its own pile. I make my way through the list, stopping when two kids have the same last name. "Are Richard and James twins?"

Amanda shakes her head, not looking up from writing another beautiful name on her high-quality name plates. "Cousins. There's actually a third cousin, too. I can't remember his name right now, but you can ask Alice."

Just then, a figure pops into the doorway. "Did I hear my name?"

"You did!" Amanda pauses to turn toward the newcomer. "She wanted to know about the Lincoln boys."

Alice makes her way over to us, holding a stack of fresh copies in one arm while pulling down a chair from the stack with the other. "James was an absolute doll last year in Kindergarten, I doubt that's changed. Richard goes by Ricky, and he will do anything for a laugh."

"And the third cousin?" I ask.

"Jeremy is..." She nods her head back and forth, scrunching up her face. "A bit of a troublemaker. Nothing major, but keep an eye on him. He will bring his cousins into his plans, too, so make sure to seat them away from each other."

"They just put cousins all in the same class? Wouldn't it be better to split them up?"

"We would if we could, but remember, there's only one class per grade here."

I do a light facepalm. "Right. That's going to take some getting used to. Anyone else I should look out for?"

"As far as student behavior goes, no. I will give you a list of academic concerns to keep an eye on; I have it written up from the end of last year. But for parents, Gabriel's mom, Mrs. Costa, can be a bit intimidating. She likes to volunteer in the classroom, and she can be really helpful, but she also does it so she can hover. Give her jobs *outside* of the room, like one-on-one reading practice in the hallway."

"This is really helpful, actually. Thanks." To be honest, I'm still fairly overwhelmed, but not nearly as much as I'd been this morning.

Alice stands up, pushing her chair back against the wall. "You are very welcome. If you have any other questions, I'm right downstairs."

Amanda puts the finishing touches on her names and blows on the last few to get the ink to dry faster. "And just like that, I have a class."

I look at mine, half-finished. These names each represent a real kid that will be in my class next Monday. Twenty-three children that I am solely responsible for over the course of an entire year. The weight of that idea hits me like a brick.

Half an hour before the end of the day, Amanda drops by my room again, backpack slung on one shoulder. She nods approvingly as she makes a 360. "Look at you! At this rate, you might not even have to come in on the weekend to be ready in time."

I look around with a frown. "Are you sure it isn't too... boring? All the cutesy classroom inspiration posts on Pinterest make me think I need to do a *lot* more."

"Don't worry about it. You can always add the cutesy stuff later. Besides, if any parents ask about your choices in decor, you can just say you're trying to promote an academic learning environment. They will eat that stuff up." She swings her backpack to her front to put her keys inside.

"Are you leaving already?" I ask, looking up at the clock.

"Yeah, Mark told me to go over early and save us a space. Want to walk with me?"

I rack my brain for what she's talking about. Is it another meeting? "Um... sure? Where are we going?"

Her shoulders sink. "Nobody's told you? Staff tradition. We go to O'Connor's Pub after the first day of work and get appetizers and drinks."

"Say less. I'm in." I scan the mess of to-be-hung decorations left all over the floor. *That is future Danielle's problem.*

We walk the three blocks to the pub—it's right where I turn off the main street to get to the school, though I've never noticed it before.

It isn't too crowded, but there are people scattered here and there. There's a long table along one wall, adjacent to a sunken area with a few couches. We place our sweaters on a few chairs and Amanda asks the two people sitting at the table how long they'll be. When she explains that we have a large group coming, they politely pick up and move to a smaller table elsewhere.

She waves at other staff members through the large window, signaling where we are, as a waitress comes to ask what we'd like. Amanda orders some IPA I don't catch the name of and I ask for the same. "He's going to get these." Amanda points to Mark as he enters the space.

"Did you get appetizers?" He asks us, pulling out his wallet.

"Not yet. We started with the important stuff."

Mark hands his credit card to the waitress while gesturing to us and all the other staff who have filed in. "I've got these two, those guys, and all of those people, too. Can we get two things of nachos, an artichoke dip, a hummus plate, and two things of fries?"

"Anything to drink?" She asks.

"I'll just have a Coke," he says before checking in with some teachers on the couches.

I lean close to Amanda and bring my voice low. "Our boss isn't drinking. Should we be drinking if he's not?"

She laughs, covering her mouth to keep with the secretive vibe we have going. "He usually does, but there's a new parent orientation tonight. If he didn't want his staff drinking, he wouldn't be taking us to a place with so much alcohol. Just don't overdo it. Not until he leaves, at least."

I get the feeling I'm going to really like this place, or at least really like Amanda. The waitress arrives with our beers and we both take a sip. I am usually not an IPA person, but this one isn't too bad. "What was this again?" I ask Amanda.

"Deschutes." She pulls over a menu and flips to the back, pointing at the name among the handful of choices from the local-ish brewery.

I take note of it, then open the menu to see what the food offerings are. As I look it over, my stomach starts to growl—just in time to see some of the appetizers coming our way. A plate of fries finds its way between me and Amanda, and a few other teachers join us to get in on them. I meet Mrs. Schumacher who teaches eighth grade and Mrs. Davis who teaches third. I also try some of the most delicious fry sauce I've ever had. *I wish Charlie would take me out more so we can find hidden gems like this.*

Mark leaves after finishing his Coke, but says everyone else is free to stay, just not on his tab. I know I'm done after this beer since I still have to drive home, but when Amanda suggests sharing some fish and chips, I decide I can stay a *little* longer. She tells me more about the fun traditions of the school, including staff field trips to the roof just to see the view. Suddenly that "never have I ever" prompt makes sense.

After splitting the check for the meal, Amanda and I walk back to the school and our cars. People are starting to show up for the orientation, so I sneak in to grab my bag from my classroom as quickly as I can. I pause before leaving, looking over all the work I have yet to do, but also incredibly proud of what I've done so far. It's going to be a great year, I just know it.

CHAPTER 3

The First Weeks of School

Alice was *not* kidding about Jeremy. My classroom management playbook was all but exhausted when I finally figured out what worked for keeping him on task. Hand-holding. Literal hand-holding. He acted like it was the worst punishment in the world, but I saw the grin he would get when I asked him to the front of the line. He just wants the attention from his teacher.

Aside from minor disruptions—shouting out, little tiffs, pushing buttons—the first two weeks went by smoothly. Too smoothly. It lulled me into a false sense of security because once that honeymoon phase was over and the kids got comfortable, I had to rethink everything. It was about that time that the review phase was over and I had to actually start *teaching* them new concepts. Now, I have to tailor lessons to each student's level. I have to juggle *everything*. Thank goodness I have Amanda and Alice to go to for guidance. Amanda is great for the "did this actually happen?" chats, while Alice gives practical advice based on what she remembers about the kids from last year. There's no way I can survive without them.

Today, we have the first Mass of the year. Usually, we go as whole school every Friday, but this week it has to be Thursday because of a funeral tomorrow. Having only gone to church three times in the past decade or so, I spent the night on YouTube refreshing myself on what to say and do. I was in middle school the last time they changed the words—"and with your spirit" instead of "and also with you" and all that. I had no idea if they switched it up again since then, so I thought it best to check.

First thing in the morning, we unpack our bags and line up to leave for the church. Thankfully, nobody has taken off their sweaters yet, as full uniform is required. Unfortunately, two kids were sent to school without sweaters in the first place. Alice, having thought ahead for me, dropped off three spare sweaters early this morning. I throw one at Tristan and one at Carter.

Tristan's fits fine, but I hear Carter's voice in a panic. "Miss Monroe!" The bottom of the sweater is almost to his knees and his fingertips are nowhere in sight.

"I am so sorry, Carter, but we're going to have to make do." I roll up his sleeves so he can at least use his hands.

As he heads back into line, he shows off his newfound fingers to his classmates, wiggling them in front of their faces as if they're the coolest thing in the world.

While crossing the street to get to the church, Irene and Alanna are busy trying to jump from one crosswalk stripe to the next. *Trying* is the operative word here because Alanna falls, taking Irene down with her. I rush out to the middle of the road to help them up and hurry them off. No scratches or scrapes, but Irene is bawling anyway. The other classes are right on our heels, so we head into the church and find a few rows with enough space for my whole class.

The kids mostly remember what to do from last year, and my refresher last night was helpful. I was smart enough to sit by Jeremy, but next time I will place myself in the middle of *all* of the students so I don't have to get up to redirect them. Lots of chatting and pew-kicking, though I don't blame them too much for the latter since their legs are too short to reach the ground. I think I hear a hymnal book ripping, too, but when I stand up to search for the culprit, all hands are empty. The art teacher steps in to sit with my class, which is good because kids keep asking if they can use the restroom, but I don't actually know where it is in this building.

By the time the Mass is over, the kids are shaking with pent-up energy, while my energy is completely spent. I let them run wild on the playground for a few minutes before I take them inside, knowing that the fresh air will do us all some good. When we make it back to class, it feels like the day is a bust because *nobody* is on task and I don't have the brainpower to figure out how to corral them. Thrown off their routine, I realize *this* is what my class would be like for a substitute. I cringe. I absolutely hated subbing for these kinds of classes. The half hour before lunch just turns into an indoor recess because I run out of ideas.

After dropping the kids off for lunch, I sit in my quiet classroom and just *breathe*. I need a serious reset before I go get them, so I put my earbuds in and play the angstiest playlist I have at full blast. If it's going to be loud, it's going to be a controlled loud. I rest my forehead on my desk and zone out as best I can, partially hoping that the decibels blasting into my ears might temporarily damage my eardrums enough to put a mute on some of the louder kids. I hear a drumming noise that is not in rhythm with the Paramore song playing and look up.

The woman standing in my doorway, knuckles resting on the door, looks ten times more put-together than I do today. I shoot a glance at the clock in the bottom corner of my computer. *12:20. Shit. I told Gabriel's mom she could meet me in my room at 12:15. This must be her.*

I rip out my earbuds and pause the music while standing to greet her. "Mrs. Costa, I am so sorry! I lost track of time."

She doesn't smile. In fact, she looks downright angry, but part of me is hopeful that it's just her normal face.

"I hope you weren't waiting there long." I reach out my hand to shake hers.

She doesn't take it, instead walking toward the back table and sitting down. "I was here exactly at 12:15. Mrs. Smith was paging you to let you know I was here, but I suppose you were too busy with your music to notice."

I sit across from her at the table. "Again, I'm sorry. It's been a long morning."

"I saw. It seems you had your hands full at Mass." There was no humor to her voice, no sympathy either.

I force a smile to my face, realizing this is not going to be a fun meeting. "Live and learn. I'm sure the next Mass will go better."

"Let's hope so."

Silence falls when I don't respond, so I change the subject. "In your email you said you wanted to talk about Gabriel's academics? From what I've seen so far, he is doing very well."

"Of course he is doing well. You're only doing Kindergarten work."

"We usually do review for a few weeks at the beginning of the year, but now we're moving into newer material—first grade material."

"I had my friend who is a teacher send me what first graders should be working on, and I see none of it in what has been sent home." She slaps a packet of paper on the table. It's a print-off from the Common Core website.

"We are going to address all the standards this year. We've even started to work on the foundational skills for some of them; I just haven't sent it home yet because I'm still—."

"Gabriel is going to need more of a challenge than this—" she gestures to the standards. "He can do most of these already. Mrs. del Rosario should have told you how gifted he is and told you what he was working on with her."

My fake smile is holding on by a fraying thread. I am exhausted, frazzled, and now feeling insulted by this woman. Her tone alone is enough to make me want to shrink back, but I have to try to look as capable as a twenty-year teaching veteran. It is too much for me to handle, and I bite back tears as I squeak out, "It looks like I need to pick up the kids from recess soon. How about I email you the plan I come up with for Gabriel?"

Mrs. Costa narrows her eyes, but accepts with a nod. She collects her purse and makes for the door, but pauses halfway there. "You know, Mark really shouldn't hire first-year teachers. It isn't fair to you or to the kids."

I sit in my chair, stunned. I manage to keep myself from crying until I see her leave the office, but then I break down. Thankfully, my desk is out of view from the door so I move over there to have myself a good, ugly cry. While I had hated finding storage spots for all the Kleenex boxes, I realize that I may get as much use out of them as the kids do. I am supposed to have this woman volunteer in my classroom regularly? I'm not sure I even want to have a conversation with her again.

I go get my students while my eyes are still red and puffy. A few have concerned looks on their faces when they see me, but they don't say anything. I think they know, though, because the afternoon goes pretty well. When kids start to get off-task, all it takes is a whisper from a classmate to get them back on track.

As we are packing up for the day, Christine approaches me with a soft smile and says, "I hope your day gets better."

I thank her, barely holding back a fresh wave of tears. These kids really are the sweetest.

After the kids are dismissed for the day, Amanda walks in with a huge grin on her face. "Man, today was a good day." Her expression falls when she sees me on the verge of tears. "What happened?" She takes a few hurried steps to me, does an about face, and snags some tissue before coming to my side.

"Mass, moms, misbehavior."

"A multitude of messy misadventures?"

I pause to admire how quickly she came up with the alliteration, then huff out the last of my sobs. "Messy. Definitely messy." I suppose I could be describing my day or my face right now.

"Which one are we starting with?" Amanda pulls out a student's chair in order to sit in front of me. "Which one sucked the most?"

"Probably the mom." I wipe the last of my snot with a tissue.

"Your mom? Is everything good with your parents?"

I can't help but give a morbid chuckle. "My mom is still securely six feet under, right where I left her a decade ago. It was Gabriel's mom."

Her back pulls off the back rest while her eyes go wide. "What did she do?"

I tell her what happened during the meeting, and she responds with appropriate gasps and interjections. When I finish, she leans back again and nods slowly. "She's learned. Last year she would say the mean things by email, but now she knows not to leave a paper trail." She gets up and heads to the stack of lined writing paper. "But you responding in email is perfect. We can work together to draft something that will shut her up."

We discuss what my plans are for advanced students, what standards we're addressing now, and how I want to frame everything. In only a half hour, we have a complete email that will hopefully appease Mrs. Costa. It mostly boils down to: "Your kid might be able to do more than Kindergarten work, but that doesn't mean he's ready for advanced first grade work. He's going to need to prove he can do what is expected of him before he gets enrichment." All in much more professional language, of course. I also make sure to say, "If you have any further questions or concerns, please feel free to email me." No way I'm inviting her into my classroom without another teacher or administrator present.

When we hit *send*, a weight was immediately lifted from my shoulders.

"Thank you so much, Amanda. It would have taken me hours to write anything like that." I look at the clock and it is just after quitting time. "And you missed your whole afternoon prep time."

"Hey, putting that mom straight now helps me next year, so consider it an investment in my own future. Now, what were the other things that were bothering you?"

"Mass and misbehavior, but I think the misbehavior came from Mass changing our routine. I was thrown so far off my game."

"Yeah, I saw you a little frazzled. Why weren't you with your buddy class?"

I stare at her blankly. "My what?"

"Your Reading Buddy class—they should sit by you at Mass. The sixth graders sit with second grade. They can help take them for bathroom breaks, model expectations, and, most importantly, sit alternating, so no two second graders and no two sixth graders sit next to each other."

"I don't have a Reading Buddy class, though."

"Yes you do! It's second and sixth, Kindergarten and eighth, and..." She bites her lip with worry, taking in a deep breath. "You and seventh. Oh my. I am so sorry. You're both new, so neither of you would have known."

"What does 'Reading Buddies' entail?"

She perks up. This topic is clearly something she loves. "It's the best half hour of the week. The big kids come to your classroom and read with your students. For my kids, the younger students are reading to the older students if they feel confident enough. This year is the best because it's my first class coming back to read." She is distracted by something and hurries to the door. "Adam! Come here for a second!"

Mr. Johnson appears in the doorway, his bag in his hand and his tie loosened around his neck. He's worn a tie every student day so far this year. It feels like a little much for a teaching job, but I have to admit the guy looks good in that middle ground between business attire and business casual. "What's up?"

"Your class and Danielle's class are Reading Buddies. Your kids will drop by once a week for a half hour to read to them. The buddies will also sit together for Masses and stuff." She says the whole spiel in one breath.

Adam's brow shoots up as I can see the stream of words processing in his mind. "Cool." He looks at me. "Want to start tomorrow? Forty-five minutes before the end of the day to give the kids time to pack up after?"

"Sure. Tomorrow at 2:15."

He points to the front door. "I gotta go to an appointment, but how about I drop by tomorrow morning so we can pair off our students?"

"Sounds great. See you bright and early tomorrow."

Adam taps the door frame twice before walking out of view.

Amanda turns around, clapping her hands together. "And just like that, Mass will be so much easier." She peeks back at the door before coming in close to me. "He's pretty cute. Are you seeing somebody?"

"Yes, I have a boyfriend. Do you?"

She lets out a short laugh. "Nope. No boyfriend here."

"You should go for it, then."

She scrunches up her face and shakes her head. "Not my type." She shrugs. "He's probably not single, anyway."

"With that smile? I doubt it." I pack up my stuff, my mood completely reversed from what it had been less than an hour ago. I really did land somewhere special.

CHAPTER 4

The Reading Buddy

"We're going to need someone really on top of things for Jeremy," I say, looking down my class list. I want to place the trickier students first.

Adam is sitting across the back table from me, his own class list in his hands. "Chase is very by-the-book. He is good at keeping his classmates on track. Maybe he'd be good?"

I write Chase-Jeremy on my notepad. "One down, twenty-two to go."

"Oh, I only have twenty. I guess three of mine will double-buddy?"

I look through and choose my six best-behaved students. "These ones will do well sharing a buddy, I think."

Adam writes the names with three of his. We continue our way through our lists with little resistance. Our classes match up so naturally, it seems. The real proof of it will happen at the end of the day, though, when the buddies actually *interact* with each other.

After our last recess, the kids are practically buzzing with a combination of excitement and nerves. I only told them that Reading Buddies would start today. I said nothing about who would be buddied-up with whom. The more outgoing kids are chomping at the bit to know who they get to hang out with, while the more reserved ones either have a wait-and-see attitude or are downright scared of meeting an older kid.

The seventh graders arrive at the door and Adam pops his head in. "Where do you want us?"

"Um... Go ahead and line up along the back and we can do introductions there."

The kids file in, but they are so much larger than my students that they don't quite fit. The line curves around the room and ends halfway down the next wall.

After going over some ground rules about appropriate book etiquette and how to be a good buddy, we announce the pairings. I save the shy ones for the end so there would be less attention on them when it was time to meet their buddy. Adam did a great job picking considerate seventh graders for my less outgoing kids.

Within five minutes, everyone finds a place in the room and settles in to start reading. My heart warms at seeing these big kids picking out their childhood favorites to share with their little buddies. I wonder if it will stay this way later in the year, or if this is going through that same honeymoon phase that other student behaviors go through.

I make my way over to my desk—the only place in the entire room without a body in it. I am not sure how many people are allowed in this room according to fire code, but in the late summer/early fall afternoon warmth, I can tell the room is going to get really warm in the next half hour. I look over to see if the windows are shut, but Adam is already over there unlatching and opening them.

"Thank you," I say when he meets me over at my desk.

"First rule of middle schoolers: keep the windows open whenever you can."

"Good to know."

A seventh grader sitting nearby calls out, "Hey, Mr. Johnson! Who's your Reading Buddy?"

Without missing a beat, he says, "Miss Monroe, obviously."

That revelation is met with a couple of *ooooh*s from the older kids, their buddies looking on in confusion.

"Yeah, yeah. You worry about your own buddies." He turns back to me and comes in close. "Don't tell them, but I made sure to save the best buddy for myself."

I squint my eyes. "And what will we be reading?"

He makes his way over to the bookshelf and comes back with a small chapter book. "How about this?" He holds out a copy of *Charlotte's Web*.

"You know, I've never actually read that."

"It's on *your* shelf."

"Yeah, I bought it at a yard sale over the summer. I haven't read most of the books in that library."

He looks at the cover, running his thumb over the title. "You know? It's actually pretty depressing from what I remember. I'll bring something for next time."

"Something less depressing?"

"Well, probably not. This book was sort of an introduction for kids into the roller coaster of emotions that come in literature."

"I wouldn't even know. I hardly ever get to read for pleasure."

His smile beams. "Now you get half an hour every week."

After a busy and exhausting week, I am excited to have the buddies come back. I need some time to just read and unwind, and my students need it, too. Adam walks in with two paperback copies of *The Hunger Games* and places one in my hands once all the kids are settled.

"I already know this story."

He raises his brow, staring straight at me with his brown eyes that, upon closer inspection, have some green to them. "But have you read the book?"

I look away, feigning embarrassment. "No. I watched the movie."

"Good. Me, too. We should probably see what the 'book is better than the movie' crowd is going on about." He sits and opens his copy.

I stare at the book, looking over the back cover and title page before closing it again.

Adam looks up. "Do you want me to read it to you?" It is hard to tell if he is joking.

"No, I think I'm alright on my own." I eye him to gauge his reaction to my response. He just shrugs and goes back to the book, so I am still not sure if he was actually offering to read to me. I open my copy and get started. Of course, I'm barely a page in before I'm interrupted by a student asking to use the restroom. As usual, it initiates a chain of students coming up to me to ask the same. I stand to announce to the class, "Please remember your buddies are only here for half an hour. If you have a bathroom *emergency*, let me know, but if you can wait until after, I'm sure your buddy would appreciate spending more time with you."

I barely have time to crack open my book before hearing a middle schooler call from somewhere in the room, "I'm sure *your* buddy would appreciate spending more time with you."

I look at Adam to see if I had heard correctly, but he is already using *the look* on someone across the room. I follow his stare and see a preteen avert his gaze and go back to pretending to be interested in his buddy's book.

Adam swivels in his chair and gives me a sympathetic smile. "Sorry about Brady. He's..."

"... a middle school boy," I conclude. "I'm just shocked he realizes teachers have social lives. You should have seen the look on Ricky's face when he saw me at the grocery store."

"Oh, this class is well aware. I have had to shut down so many questions about my personal life."

"Like what?" I ask, leaning in closer.

"Where I live, how much I make, who my favorite student is, if I'm single..."

"I hardly even know you and I can answer those. Since you're a first-year teacher, you *basically* live in your classroom, you make *not enough*, your favorite student is *obviously* Brady, and you're—" I glance at his left hand, which has no ring, then look at his gorgeous, amused smile, "—probably not single?"

He shakes his head, closing his eyes and sighing. "You are a horrible guesser. You got *one* right."

I click my tongue. "Brady's your favorite?"

"Obviously." He manages a straight face for a beat before breaking into a stifled laugh that takes him a few seconds to get under control. "No. We don't make enough."

"You don't basically live at school? I feel like I should bring a sleeping bag for the nights I stay late to prep for the next week."

"I leave before you basically every day. That is, your light is usually still on when I drive off. I do most of my prep at home, on my couch, with The Office playing in the background."

"Ugh, I wish I could do that, but my boyfriend requires complete silence." I freeze. *Did I just let it slip that I am living with my boyfriend? Shit. Think of a reason he'd be over frequently. Think.* "He works at my place because I have better internet. I would need to wait for him to leave to get to half-watch sitcoms."

"Bummer." He looks down at his watch. "Oh, wow. We are over on time and I've barely read anything."

"I got, like, three paragraphs." I stand, clapping a rhythm that my students recognize as a call to attention. "Alright, first graders, please thank your buddy and put away your books! We are packing up once they go, so if you have a job this week, please start on your tasks!"

Adam's voice booms in the near-silent room. "And seventh grade, thank your buddies and line up by the door. First thing when we get back to the classroom, write your homework in your planner."

When he's done, I hand him my book, but he pushes it back to me.

"Keep it. Maybe you'll have a chance to read some this weekend."

I look down at the book. I really did want to read it when I was younger; I just never found the time. Maybe this would be a good way to de-stress. "I doubt it, but I'll leave it in my bag just in case."

"Same time next week?"

"Yep! And we can plan for the next all-school Mass, too."

"Looking forward to it." He shoots me that grin and I realize that I'm looking forward to it, too.

CHAPTER 5

The Books the Buddies Read

After getting the buddies started the next week, Adam sits down across from me with a guilty look on his face.

"Did you accidentally read the whole thing in one sitting, too?" I ask, holding up my copy of *The Hunger Games*.

He eases into his chair, rubbing his hands down his face. "I did. I thought I was about to owe you an explanation."

I wave him off. "No need. I loved the detail the book went into that the movie just couldn't capture. I went back and re-watched the movie this weekend, too. I forgot how good it was." It helped that Charlie was so engrossed in his video games that he didn't try to pull me away from my reading, but I don't go into that.

"So, what do we do next? The next *Hunger Games* book or do we go for other young adult books we somehow never got around to?"

I point my finger at him in warning. "Don't you dare suggest *Twilight*."

He holds up his hands in surrender. "I wouldn't dream of it. The only redeeming thing from the movies was the dad."

"Bella's dad or Edward's?"

He considers for a moment before his deadpan reply. "Charlie."

I laugh, remembering that I, too, loved the clue-less-dad-slash-grumpy-cop vibe that Charlie Swan gave off. Part of me wonders if he is the same in the books, or if it was all the actor's touch. Then again... "How do you know the name of the dad from Twilight off the top of your head?"

"My last girlfriend made me watch all the movies with her."

"Wow. It must have been true love." I press my hand over my heart and give an exaggerated, swooning sigh.

He holds up his left hand, turning it in the air, while making eye contact. His expression makes it blatantly clear that he is unamused.

"Damn, apparently not." I shrink back before I notice the middle schooler closest to us has stopped reading and is looking at me funny. *Oh, shit. I just swore.* "I'm sorry," I whisper to her, before miming zipping my lips.

When I turn back, Adam is barely containing his laughter. He takes a stabilizing breath before turning to his student and saying, "I've heard you slip more than once. I think we can give Miss Monroe some grace this time."

The young lady rolls her eyes before going back to the book.

"It's not like we *need* to be married at our ages, right?" I ask, thinking about Charlie—my boyfriend, not Bella's dad. He and I won't be married at any age. The realization stings. But Adam can't be more than 26, even if teaching was a career change for him.

"No, but I was pretty close at one point. Waste of two years."

"It can't be that bad. You must have learned something from that relationship that will help in your future ones."

He raises his brow. "Yeah, I learned lots of red flags for cheating."

"Well," I say, pausing for a deep breath, "that sucks and anything I say is clearly not helping. Should we get back to books before I look like even more of an—" I look down to be sure the young lady is still reading before spelling under my breath, "—A-S-S?"

He smiles and proves that his eye rolling ability rivals his students'. "I have the second *Hunger Games* book in my classroom. I can drop it off for you after dismissal."

After school, I am buried in writing projects. It wouldn't be so hard to grade if their letters were all at least facing the right way. Alice said I would get used to reading the sloppy penmanship and invented spelling, but it is basically a new language.

Adam appears in my doorway holding two copies of *Catching Fire*. "The school library had a copy, too, so we both get one." He holds out the less-battered one to me.

"Thanks. It will be so nice to read something that I can actually comprehend." I gesture to the mess on my desk. "I love these kids, but they either write virtually nothing or they ramble on about goodness-knows-what."

He picks up the paper on top, and I watch his lips as he tries to sound out the words. "I got nothing."

I hold up the book. "I will probably read this whole thing over the weekend just to prove to myself I can, in fact, read."

And so I did.

CHAPTER 6

The Parent

The last full week of October, we have another staff get-together at O'Connor's. Amanda waits for me to finish grading the kids' second Math test before we leave, and the results leave a smile on my face. They actually understood what I taught them. This wasn't review anymore, this was *new* stuff and they crushed it.

We walk the three blocks to the pub and find all of our coworkers already seated in the worn leather chairs. Mark gets the waitress' attention, pointing at us and then at himself. Apparently, he is covering the first round again. My empty wallet thanks him.

"How much does he make that he can just buy everyone drinks every month?" I ask as Amanda and I find a table near the group.

"Oh, it's not *his* money. His wife would be furious if that were the case. No, the parent's club gives him a discretionary fund."

The waitress arrives to take our drink orders. We both order a beer—Amanda gets something from Deschutes while I have a Guinness to make up for accidentally skipping lunch. It's basically a meal-replacement beer, right? We tack on an order of fries with Mark's permission.

"Do the parents know he spends the fund on alcohol?" I whisper after the waitress leaves.

"Do they know?" She laughs, then tilts her head in the direction of a table of men. "One of those guys is married to the parent's club president, one to the secretary, and the other two are school dads, too." She scrunches her brow. "Actually, I think one of your students belongs to the guy in the plaid."

The waitress returns with our beers, promising to be right back with the fries. I take a sip as I stare at the dads. I can't connect which student the dad belongs to until Alice comes over, her head low and voice even lower.

"Do you recognize the dad over there?" she asks, a secret behind her smile, as she steals a chair from another table.

"No. Amanda says he's a parent of one of my students, but I can't figure out which one."

"His wife made you cry your second week here."

My jaw drops. "That's *Mr.* Costa?" I won't lie. He is an attractive man. The dark hair, thick beard, and the way his muscles just barely fit in his sleeves make him look like a sexy lumberjack. As much as I dislike Mrs. Costa, I can't help but envy her a bit in this moment.

"The one and only. Watch out for him at school or church events with drinking. He can get a little...animated."

My interest is piqued, but I don't dare ask for more information. I'm not sure I want to think of dad gossip every time I look at Gabriel—though, part of me thinks it would be better than thinking of his mom. When she isn't asked more about it, Alice leaves, looking somewhat disappointed. Perhaps I'll ask her for stories at the end of the year.

I check my phone. Charlie has the car and was supposed to text me with a time he would be able to pick me up. I still haven't heard from him, so I send him another reminder message.

Pretty soon, all the teachers with kids of their own have to leave. Others trickle out, too, leaving Adam, Amanda, and me.

Amanda regales us with tales of her first year teaching as we each order another beer. Her first class, this year's sixth graders, was quite the interesting group.

"You know, Michael and Samantha have been making doe-eyes at each other nonstop during science class," Adam notes when the two come up in the story. "I feel bad for their lab partners—they can never focus on anything but each other."

"Oh, I know. When sixth comes in to read with second grade, those two are placed on opposite ends of the room." Amanda shrugs. "I never would have guessed it four years ago, though. Those two hardly interacted—positively or negatively."

I take out my phone again—still no messages. "Do you guys get good signal here? I'm supposed to be getting a text but nothing is coming through even though I have full bars."

Adam looks at his phone. "I got a text from my mom two minutes ago."

Amanda elbows him playfully. "*Aww.* Texting your mom on a Friday night."

I frown at my phone. "Do you two want another beer? I'm going to grab something after I make a quick call."

"Can you get me a water?" Amanda asks. "I'll have to drive home pretty soon."

"I walk to work, so surprise me," Adam says before finishing the last of his current pint.

I slip out the front door, stepping away from the noise, and call Charlie. He doesn't answer. I didn't count the rings, but it felt like it was too short to have gone to voicemail on its own. "Hey Charlie, can you please either text or call me back? You are my ride home and I am not sure how much longer people are going to hang around. Thanks. Love you." I end the call and let out a sigh before heading back in to the bar.

I order the water, then decide on rum and coke for me and Adam. Neither of us is driving and I'm in a bit of a bad mood, so why not? As I move to hand my card to the bartender, I hear a voice over my shoulder.

"Let me get this."

The speech is a bit slurred. I turn around to see dark hair and flannel—Mr. Costa—and he looks... well, like he's been at the pub for a while.

"No, thank you, Mr. Costa. I can get my own drink."

"No!" His voice is nearly a shout. "I insist." He hands his card to the bartender, but does so on the other side of me so his arm is draped over my shoulders. When his card is taken, his arm stays there.

I tap my card on the bar, trying to get the bartender's attention. "Please, don't let him pay for me." When he looks at me, I open my eyes wide, trying to express my discomfort. I hope my silent plea is enough.

Mr. Costa makes no move to take his card back, but addresses the bartender, too. "No girl that looks like this should pay for her own drinks. You should have seen the picture she sent in her—" he pauses for a burp, "—welcome back to school message."

I think back to that email. It was just a picture of me and my dad making cookies in his kitchen last Christmas. Suddenly, it is no longer my favorite picture. *That explains how he knows who I am.*

The bartender holds Mr. Costa's card in front of him. "Sir, she would like to pay for her own drinks."

Mr. Costa turns to me, his face uncomfortably close to mine. I can see every pore on his face and can smell the whiskey on his breath. "It's the least I can do for putting up with my little brat all day."

I let out an awkward laugh. "Gabriel is an absolute angel in class. If anything, I should be buying *you* a drink for raising such a sweet boy." *Please let this be enough to diffuse this.*

More of his weight presses down on my shoulders as he seems to use me for balance. "Well, then how about a drink to make up for having to deal with my bitch wife?"

At this point, I am doing everything in my power not to shake. Whether it's from fear or anger, I'm not sure, but my body is telling me something is very wrong, and my mind is having a flashback to a college experience I'd rather forget. "Mr. Costa, I'm going to need you to stop."

"What? Because I mentioned my wife?" He brings his voice down and whispers in my ear. "You do more for me than she does, Miss Monroe."

The way he says my name makes bile rise in my throat.

The bartender looks directly into my eyes. "Do you need me to call someone?"

What good would that do? Charlie isn't even picking up. Oh, does he mean the police? I don't want to call the police on a parent two months into my first teaching contract. "No, thank you." I try to push away from Mr. Costa, but his fingers clutch onto my arm, holding me firm. "Please let go, Mr. Costa." I try to sound clear and firm, but my nerves have moved into my vocal cords.

His lips are hovering just above my cheek and I can feel his breath on my skin as he says, "Call me Felix."

I'm more forcibly trying to break away when a voice comes from the other side. "Sir, let go of Miss Monroe. Now."

I look to see Adam there, towering over us, his face more stern than I had ever seen before.

Mr. Costa pulls me closer, nearly making me fall in the process. *Down. I haven't tried down yet.* I let my knees collapse under me, but despite being intoxicated, Mr. Costa's reflexes are fast enough to catch me on the way down.

"What would you do without me here to look out for you?" He asks with a suggestive grin.

I look back to Adam and mouth the word "help." I see Amanda on the other side of the bar on her phone, staring at the scene with eyes wide.

Adam grabs at Mr. Costa's hand on my arm and pries his fingers off one by one. When I am free of the grip, I move around Adam, taking a position a few steps behind him to watch what happens next.

Adam is holding tight to Mr. Costa's left hand—the one that had been holding me. Mr. Costa tries to shake free of the grip, but can't. Instead, he uses his right hand to swing a fist toward Adam's face. It makes contact with his jaw before he can move out of the way, but not before I see Principal Mark appear near the front door.

The whole pub is dead silent, so Mark's voice can be heard across the room. "Mr. Costa, I suggest you leave immediately." He looks at the other men who were sitting at the table. "Mr. Frank, Mr. Vincent, please see that he gets home."

The other dads move to pull Mr. Costa away. He is shaking the hand he just punched Adam with, mumbling curses. Mark walks over to me and Adam turns around, both asking at the same time, "Are you alright?"

I take a shaky breath and shake my head. What the hell just happened?

Adam holds out his arm next to me. "Let's get you to the couches. I can help if you need it."

I nod, but don't take his arm. I appreciate the gesture, but I don't want to touch *anyone* right now. He walks with me down the two stairs to the couches. Mark follows with a glass of water and a glass of ice.

Amanda beats us there. "Oh my gosh, Danielle, are you okay? Sit down. Sit." She takes the water from Mark and sets it down in front of me.

I pick up the water with a shaking hand, somehow not spilling it as I take a long sip. When I set it back down I ask, "Is this what Alice meant by 'animated?'"

"Oh, God, no. Last year he got loud and stumbled around at a few parents' club meetings, and spent too much at the school auction, but *nothing* like this. We would have told you if we had known he was like this."

Mark and Adam sit across from us, Mark pouring ice into a cloth napkin and twisting it off so Adam can use it as an ice pack. "Will you want to press charges?"

Adam holds it against the side of his jaw. "Well, if this swells, it might interfere with my modeling gig this weekend, so maybe sue for lost wages."

Mark looks at him, unamused. "I need to know if you're joking right now."

Adam holds up his free hand. "Yes, it was a joke. Not a good time for it. I'm sorry. No, I probably won't press charges, but I think you should be asking Danielle the same question."

They all look at me and I shrink back into the couch. "I don't know? I'm not sure I want to go through that whole process." I press my eyes closed and shake my arm. It still feels like his hand is gripping my muscle. "But I don't think I want to be around him again."

Mark takes out his phone and starts typing out something. "Absolutely. He will not be allowed at school events until you give me the word. We will also tell mom that she will be the only one allowed to parent-teacher conferences next month." He taps the phone a few more times, then ends with one flourishing tap. "There. I drafted an email to send later tonight. If you do decide to press charges, you can do that yourself or I am happy to help you out with that process. Either way, I would appreciate knowing what you decide so we can be prepared."

I give him a slow nod, still processing everything. Then I stop. "How did you know to come back?"

"Amanda called. She knew I would still be at the school and told me to run over as quickly as I could." He stands suddenly. "Which reminds me, I'm parked in a loading zone. I'll be right back." He rushes to the door, shoving his hand in his pocket to get his keys.

"How's your arm?" Amanda asks. "It looked like he had a death grip on it."

I rub my left arm, just below my shoulder. "Yeah, he had it pretty tight. I don't think it will bruise or anything, though."

"If it does, you should take pictures, in case you change your mind about going to the police."

"I will." I turn to Adam. "And you should take a picture of whatever becomes of *that*." I gesture to his chin. "One to keep in case you want to file a police report, two so I can see how much I should be thanking you."

Adam adjusts his ice pack. "I don't think it will be too bad. One of the advantages of being tall is that it's hard to get a good shot. I mean, if he wanted to give me a black eye he would have had to ask me to bend down first."

I laugh at the image. "Or he could climb up on a barstool." It feels weird to joke about it, but if I think too much about how serious it was, I might shut down again.

After a short silence, Amanda asks, "Do you want me to give you a ride home? I saw you got dropped off this morning."

I look at my phone once more. Still no messages or missed calls. "Yeah, that would be great. Thanks. Adam, are you good to head home on your own?"

"Yeah, I'm just going to stay for a bit and talk to the bartender."

We collect our things, but before going I look over my shoulder at Adam and say, "Thanks for rescuing me."

He waves it off. "Nobody messes with my Reading Buddy."

CHAPTER 7

The Invitation

My heart flutters when I see the long, fancy writing on the front of the envelope. The squeal that comes from my throat is much louder than I anticipate.

Charlie grunts in question, not looking away from his computer screen.

"I think this is Carl's wedding invitation!" I tear open the envelope as quickly as I can while still preserving the calligraphy. We got the Save the Date for the Seattle nuptials ages ago, but I have been craving more details. Carl was always over-the-top back in college, so I fully expect his wedding to have that same vibe. Three papers fall out and I immediately reach for the invitation itself. My jaw drops when I see the location. "They're getting married at Brackhill Manor."

"So?" Charlie asks, finally turning his chair around.

"So, it's basically a castle! Can you imagine having a wedding in a castle?" I press the invitation to my heart, feigning a swoon.

"I can't imagine having a wedding anywhere. They're just dumb ways for vendors to monetize the government forcing their way into relationships."

"Well, I can't wait to celebrate Carl and Anthony with their family and friends in a beautiful venue." I grab the RSVP. "Can I count you as my plus one?"

He scoffs. "No." His tone is as if I was insane for even asking.

"No?" I ask, hoping it is some kind of joke.

"I told you when you got the card about holding the day—I don't like Carl. Why would I want to go to his wedding?"

"Maybe because it's a fun date night for us at a beautiful location? We can make a whole weekend of it, go to some breweries nearby, stay in a nice hotel."

"You say that like I don't have responsibilities here to take care of."

I want to gesture around me to the lack of responsibilities he has, but I stop myself. No use fighting. "Then you expect me to go alone?"

"Of course not. You should go with a girl friend. What about that Miss Finch from work?"

I smile at his remembering something from my life, until...

"She has a car, right? I'll need to keep ours here just in case." He turns back to his computer, effectively ending the conversation.

My shoulders droop, the image of a fun weekend with my boyfriend in Seattle erased. I was supposed to do dishes after getting the mail, but I want to remove myself from the room for a bit. I grab my coat and walk outside. It's a sunny day, albeit a bit chilly. Some of our neighbors are walking their dog, Buster. Don't ask me what the neighbors' names are, but I can tell you the name of every dog who walks in this area. I give a polite wave before reaching into my pocket for my phone.

Danielle: Any chance you want to be my plus one to a wedding in Seattle at the start of Spring Break?

I put my phone away, turning toward the park that isn't too far. I hardly go two steps before my phone buzzes.

> Amanda: Absolutely! I'm flattered you'd ask!
> Amanda: As long as I'm back by the Tuesday of break for my trip to Michigan we're good.
> Danielle: It's on Saturday, the day after school gets out, so I think it will work out perfectly!

I continue with my walk, enjoying the crisp air, the last of the red and brown leaves clinging to the trees. The park is quiet compared to the chaos that takes place in summer. Once spring rolls around, there will be the farmer's market, summer camp trips, and so many families trying to fill time, but for now, almost the whole park is mine.

I take time to re-imagine the weekend as I walk. No longer am I introducing old acquaintances to Charlie and having him talk about the books he's written and the process of trying to land a book deal; now I get to dance all night with someone who *wants* to be there. We can adventure around the city, acting like lost tourists, instead of spending the entire time looking for places "only locals go" like Charlie prefers. The dopey grin on my face suddenly disappears as I realize—I just invited my Catholic co-worker to a gay wedding.

I stop walking in the middle of the path. *Would going to this wedding be against Catholic teaching? Should I uninvite her?* I shake my head, remembering that Amanda is way too chill to be weird about something like this. Maybe she'll still want to go. But then again, I've only known her a few months and telling her the truth about the wedding could give her ammunition to possibly get me fired.

I force myself to start walking again. No good thinking happens while standing still. Maybe I can slip something about gay marriage into conversation one day and see how she reacts. Maybe I can tell her that Charlie ended up being able to go and wants to be my plus one—but then how do I get to the wedding with no car?

By the time I arrive home, my mood is right back where it started when I left. Charlie is in the bathroom, so I peek at his computer screen. As expected, he is not on his manuscript. He is, however, on a website for rentals in...*Indiana?* I hear the sink turn off, so I scurry away from the desk, taking off my coat by the door.

Charlie looks surprised to see me. "I thought you were out for the evening."

My head cocks. "No, I just went for a walk. Do you have plans tonight?"

He stretches his hands out to the computer. "You're looking at them."

"Looking for apartments?" I ask. I don't want to admit the level of snooping I did.

"Looking for cheaper places to live. Oregon is too expensive for us now. After this school year, I think we should find a place more in our price range."

I huff. "This isn't a good time for me to think about a move. I have a lot going on right now. Can we put a pin in this idea?"

"You don't worry about it. I'll keep looking into it and let you know what I find when you're ready."

There's the sweet guy I'm dating. "Thank you," I say as I kiss him on the cheek before I head to our room to work on lesson plans for the next week.

When Monday rolls around, I have my plan. I bring Amanda an iced coffee with one sugar and a splash of coconut milk, then sit down at the student desk nearest to hers to pull out the wedding invitation.

She nearly spits out her coffee as she reads it. "You didn't tell me it was a *gay* wedding!"

My heart sinks while picking up its pace at the same time. "So...you don't want to go?"

She looks at me with wide eyes. "Of *course* I want to go! Some of the most fun weddings I've been to were gay weddings." She looks back at the invite. "And it's at a *manor*. That sounds fancy. Attire: formal? We're going dress shopping, right?"

I let out my breath. "Yeah, it's basically a castle. Carl was never going to have a plain wedding, and he's marrying a guy from a pretty well-off family, so I expect it to be quite the event." I take the card back from her. "Honestly, I was a little worried about asking my Catholic co-worker to a gay wedding."

Amanda bites her lip in a smile before bringing her coffee to her lips. "Oh, girl. If only you knew..." She pushes back her chair and grabs a stack of papers. "Can I walk you to your room? I've got to make some copies."

We decide to make a day of dress shopping sometime after the craziness of the holidays. Amanda says she won't try on dresses before then because, apparently, the school families love to bring in Christmas treats for the teachers and we can expect to gain at least an inch.

And suddenly I can't wait for the holidays.

CHAPTER 8

The Christmas Program

Amanda wasn't kidding. The sheer volume of sweets I am taking home tonight is insane. Not to mention the gift cards and the wine. Yes, *wine*. Three bottles of red so far, and not the cheap stuff either. It will all be coming home with me once the Christmas program is over.

Oh, boy. The Christmas program. It feels like one of those events that you can't actually prepare for. Everyone just tells you where to be and a rough estimate of when. Anything that happens beyond that is out of your control. My students would be dropped off at the lunch room where we would hang out until it is our turn to go. That is all I know.

Alice, Amanda, and I are camped out by the door waiting for a runner to come get one of our classes while we talk about our plans for Christmas break as the kids watch cartoons.

Alice looks at her watch. "My parents should be landing in Honolulu now."

"Honolulu?" Amanda asks. "Are there no direct flights from the Philippines?"

Alice's eyes widen. "From Manila to Portland? I'm not sure it's a very high-demand route. Plus they are going to take the same route back when they leave in February and spend a few days in Hawaii."

"I could use some Hawaiian sun in February," I muse as I look out the basement windows. It isn't quite snowing—more like giant dollops of slush falling from the sky. Very wet, very cold, very northwest. A laugh from the kids breaks me from my trance. "What about you, Amanda? Staying local this Christmas?"

"I am escaping to southern California. My roommate's family lives down there, so we're going to spend Christmas with them and hit up Disneyland."

"Have you been before?" I ask. I always love giving tips for first-timers.

"Yeah, loads of times, but never at Christmas. I can't wait to see it all lit up and decorated."

I smile, remembering the artificial snow and the Christmas lights, even the Nightmare Before Christmas overlay on the Haunted Mansion ride. I used to go to Disneyland a lot with my mom as a kid; she was definitely one of the original "Disney Adults." I even went a few times with friends as I got older, but Charlie doesn't like Disney as a company, so we do other things for vacations—mostly road trips and visiting friends.

A tap on my back pulls me from my thoughts. Wow, I must be tired with all of this zoning out. Good thing break starts once this program is over.

A seventh grader is standing behind me. I can't remember her name, but she is Ruth's Reading Buddy. "Mrs. Finch, Mr. Johnson told me to come get Kindergarten."

I move to the side and gesture to Alice. "You're up!"

Two class chants and thirty seconds later, Alice has her class lined up and heading out the door. I am amazed that these kids just started school three and a half months ago—they have their routines down pat. "She's amazing," I remark to Amanda.

"She's good, but she's also been doing this for ten years. Give it time—you'll get there, too." We watch them leave, admiring the glittery dresses and Christmas outfits on these little five-year-olds. One little boy even has on a full suit. Amanda angles her body toward the kids in the lunchroom again, but continues the conversation. "What about you? Where are you headed for break?"

I shake my head. "Making the super long drive to Hillsboro to see my dad."

She clutches her chest, rolling her eyes. "How will you ever survive the half-hour drive?"

"I will need at least three bathroom stops."

"And probably a trip to Dutch Bros just to stay awake."

"My boyfriend will have to take over driving when my legs start to cramp."

Amanda turns to me with a wide-eyed interest. "The boyfriend spending holidays with dad? So this is serious..."

I shrug. "We've been together, like, four years. His family lives in Florida, so he just hangs out here."

Amanda perks up. "Disney *World* at Christmas, though."

I decide not to mention his dislike of the company and instead say, "Not the right part of Florida."

"So, like, Miami?"

"Tallahassee."

She nods in understanding.

We watch the movie for a bit, until Brady comes to get second grade, and it is just my class waiting. I take some time to do a head count and realize a few kids didn't make it tonight—they probably already started on their holiday plans. Some of the girls have their hair done in curls and bows. Their parents must have started getting them ready the moment they got out of school. Some of the boys have gel in their hair, but that doesn't stop Carter's cowlick from sticking straight up in the back. I see Jeremy poking at Ricky, so I move over to the side of the room where he can see me watching. Proximity is key with him.

Not long after, it is our turn to head over. Irene bolts up to run and hug Addison, who is the person who came to walk us over and her Reading Buddy.

Addison looks a bit frazzled. "I didn't know where you guys were. I think you need to be over there *right now*."

A surge of panic washes through my chest as I get everyone in line. "Alright, first graders! Walk quickly but safely, no splashing in any puddles, voices level zero when we enter the church, and don't forget to smile and sing loud!" I nod to Addison to guide us out while I take up the caboose to make sure nobody falls behind, which, of course some do because their parents put them in kitten heels they've never worn before or dress shoes with no traction.

When we make it into the church, the music teacher is at the piano playing sing-alongs. This is not part of the program. How late are we? I rush to get the kids on the risers and tuck out of the way as fast as I can, trying to hide in a sea of teachers standing on the side.

Mr. Johnson leans down and whispers just next to my ear, "Get lost?"

I give him a light elbow to the side. "No. Addison *just* got there."

"Oh, shoot. I'm sorry." He reaches behind him to grab something, then my shoulders are covered in a nice suit coat.

I am about to throw it off of me when I realize how cold I actually am. The lunch room was hot with three classes in it, but as classes left it did start to cool off significantly. The heater must have been turned off for break. Then we walked through near-freezing temperatures to get here, but I must not have registered it in my panic and embarassment of being so late. I get a whiff of an earthy smell from the fibers; not musky, but warm—almost woodsy. I pull the coat over me more securely as my students start singing.

I wouldn't say the performance of Silent Night is particularly *good*, but it sure is *sweet*. Some of the kids are terribly shy and I can see that they are barely mouthing the words, but right in the center of the pack Jeremy is belting it out, helping carry the whole performance. He is *loving* it. James and Christine have giant grins on their faces when they see their parents in the crowd, which is a giant mass of bodies in the pews. Ruth and Irene started off nervous, but now that they are holding hands they are singing with confidence. I think I need this as a last memory of these kids before break, instead of the stress of getting ready for two weeks off. Now they will live as little angels in my mind as I enjoy my relative freedom.

When my class is done, all of the other classes come back for the finale—Joy to the World. Everyone is singing loud and proud for the first verse, but it seems like some forget the second and most forget the third. I, for one, am shocked that there even *is* a third verse, having never heard it before.

When the applause is over and Mark makes the final announcements, I start to take off the coat, but Adam stops me. "You have to walk back to the building, I'll come get it from you later."

Alice, Amanda, and I gather all of our kids into one massive group and herd them back over to the lunchroom, which has dropped probably ten degrees since we left. Parents start lining up at the door to sign their kids out and start on their vacations. It takes only fifteen minutes to get nearly fifty kids checked out.

Ruth's mom is the last to arrive, having collected her three other kids first. As she is getting Ruth's coat on, she nods to the suit coat that I am now wearing properly. "You and Mr. Johnson seemed to be cozy during the performance—Naomi, go stop your brothers from ruining their nice pants!" Her oldest daughter runs off to stop the boys from roughhousing by the playground.

I shrink into the coat a bit, feeling the lining shift against the skin on my arms and back. I'm not sure how to interpret that. Was wearing his coat inappropriate? Did it go against some custom hidden deep inside the Bible somewhere? "He was just being a gentleman."

She smiles at me, dropping my feeling that it had been a judgmental statement. "He seems like a good guy. Naomi really likes him for science." She looks over her shoulder to her other three kids, then turns back to me, "Yep, they're all still alive. Merry Christmas!"

"Merry Christmas." I close the door against the biting cold. I wouldn't be surprised if it snowed properly tonight, though snow before Christmas was almost unheard of here. I head over to my purse in the corner and pull out my phone. Five missed calls and a dozen texts, all from Charlie. I scroll through in a panic, thinking something must have happened.

Charlie: what time do you need me to pick you up?

What? I told him before I left and *put a note on the fridge.*

Charlie: plz respond
Charlie: or ignore me. fine
Charlie: wow. what did I even do to deserve this?
Charlie: you even want me to pick you up?
Charlie: answer your texts
Charlie: Eddie wants to go out tonight
Charlie: he needs to know if I'm going
Charlie: whatever. I'm going
Charlie: found the post-it. still going out because you aren't responding
Charlie: its not raining anymore. you should be fine to walk.

I stare at my phone in shock. He's just going to leave me to walk in basically freezing temperatures? I pull up his number as Amanda walks over to check in on me. I wave her off and whisper "Merry Christmas" as she grabs her stuff to leave.

"Hello?" Charlie's voice is joined by a cacophony of voices having indistinct conversations behind him.

"Hi, sorry I couldn't respond, I was working. I didn't even have my phone with me for most the night."

"What?" he shouts. "I can't hear you, but at least I answer my phone when you call."

"Seriously?" I whisper under my breath, then shift to shouting in hopes he can hear me. "I'm done for the night and I would appreciate a ride home! It's too cold to walk!"

He is yelling so loud I have to hold the receiver away from my ear. "Sorry, still can't hear you! Text me!" He hangs up.

I take a deep breath, but my hands are shaking as I bring my phone in front of me to text. As I'm about to start writing, I hear a knock on the open door.

"Is everything okay?" Adam asks, carrying a large, wrapped present under his arm.

"Yeah," I start, then my breath catches and half a sob slips out. "No." I start to take off the coat, but he holds my shoulder, pinning it to me.

"Keep it on. My car takes a bit to warm up, so you might want it."

I grimace. "You heard that?"

"I did, and I am going to stop myself from commenting on it, but I am going to insist I give you a ride home." He hands me the gift. "But only after you open what I came to give you."

I look at the present. It would be very generous to assume an adult wrapped this. "For me? From you?"

He shrugs. "We have two weeks off. I thought you might need something to read during all of that downtime."

My interest is sufficiently piqued. I grab at one of the wrinkled edges and pull to reveal a black box—a book set of some kind. Another tear reveals some white letters, and my heart sinks. Yet another pull and the words *Twilight Saga* are revealed. I look up, not even trying to hide how unamused I am.

Adam bursts out laughing. "I couldn't help it."

"You seriously expect me to spend my entire Christmas break reading about Bella pining over Edward?" I can't help but let out a chuckle, too.

He gestures to the half-opened gift. "Keep opening."

Two more tears and I can see the book spines. They are a series of bold colors with a young man on the top of each. I let out a genuine laugh in relief. "You took the Percy Jackson series and..." I trail off in a sigh, dragging my free hand down my face.

"...put them in a Twilight book set box. Goodwill let me buy just the box for a buck. I couldn't help it." He holds out his elbow for me to take. "Come on, let's get you home."

When I sit in his car, I am surrounded by that same woodsy smell. I look around for a source—maybe an air freshener or bottle of cologne—but find nothing. When he starts the car, he hands me his phone with Spotify pulled up.

"It's not that long of a drive," I say.

"We can still get a song or two in. Plus, the song you pick will tell me a lot about you."

I narrow my eyes and hide my smirk as I search for Muse and play Supermassive Black Hole.

When he realizes the connection, he gives me a side eye. "You've got jokes."

I shimmy deeper into my seat, quite pleased with myself. It doesn't hurt that it is actually a good song, despite being in a certain movie we both love to hate.

We pull up in front of my place and I hand him back his phone, which is now playing through other Muse songs and is currently on a song called Starlight. His hand grazes mine as he takes his phone and we make eye contact. Something in the back of my head screams that this would be the perfect time to kiss him, and something in the front my mind agrees, but before I can do anything, Adam smiles and says, "Merry Christmas."

I give a sheepish grin in return and mumble out a "Merry Christmas" before getting out of the car, my face flush.

CHAPTER 9

The Dress

"Get in, loser! We're going shopping!"

I pause on my front steps, my mouth agape.

Amanda's eyes widen in horror from inside her car. "Oh, no. I am so sorry! It's a quote from a movie, I wasn't actually calling you—"

I start to laugh as I make my way to the passenger side. "It's fine! *Mean Girls*, yeah, I've seen it. I've just never heard you say anything mean."

"Oh, I assure you I am *full* of surprises." She wiggles her eyebrows before grabbing the clutch. "To the outlets?"

I dramatically buckle my seatbelt before echoing, "To the outlets."

We drive out of the city to one of the nearby outlet malls. We considered driving into Washington for some of their stores, but their sales tax is disgusting.

Amanda has a late-2000s playlist going and I hold back from singing along to the songs of my childhood until she turns to me saying, "Sorry, I can't help it," and then begins *belting* the chorus to Year 3000 by the Jonas Brothers. I enthusiastically join her.

When the song ends, I bring up the most important question. "Alright, which Jonas brother did you have a crush on?"

She scrunches up her face, thinking. "I don't think I ever had a *crush* on any of them, but my favorite was definitely Nick."

"Yes. Same. I'm glad we are on the same page here because there is no other choice."

She shrugs. "I mean, now that they're older, Kevin does seem to have a good head on his shoulders."

"I guess, but it's *Nick Jonas*." I would not stand for this slander. "And considering that they were child stars, I would say they all turned out pretty good."

Amanda just shakes her head and laughs as she pulls into the parking lot.

I usually have a hard time with shopping. My opinion of my body has never been the best, so staring at myself in mirrors to critique how I look can sometimes lead to some less-than-ideal self-talk. Let's just say that Amanda would not stand for that.

I look myself over in the floor-length mirror in the changing room. The green dress hugs my love handles a little too tightly. "You were right about the sweets. This extra weight looks so gross on me."

"No. I am not allowing you to say that *anything* about my friend is gross," she says, her finger pointed up in a reprimanding gesture. She turns me to the side. "It is not your job to look good in the dress. It is the dress' job to look good on you. If this isn't it, then this isn't it, but say one good thing about how you look in this one."

I suck in my gut, then exhale and let it rest naturally. I guess it isn't *too* bad. "I like the color."

"Yes! It brings out the color in your eyes." She hands over another green dress. "Same color, different cut. Let's go."

"What about yours?" I ask, reaching back to unzip my current dress.

"Pshht, I look good in everything. I'm just trying stuff on for comfort at this point, and this one hinders range of motion." She does one of those disco-pointing moves. "I will not let attire stand between me and the dance floor."

At this point I realize two things: that one day I want to have Amanda's confidence and that I definitely invited the right person to the wedding.

We go through a few more dresses and my confidence grows with each one, especially now that I'm looking for a positive for each instead of focusing on what I don't like.

"So are we walking out with any of these?" Amanda asks, holding up my stack of dresses.

I didn't *love* any of them, but I also don't want to go to another store and waste time now that Amanda already found her dress. "That last one wasn't so bad." I begin to reach for it.

Amanda pulls the stack away. "That is a 'no,' then. We are finding you a dress that you love."

"Really, Amanda. It's fine. You're set and we can just go."

"Really, Danielle, it's not fine because this is our first stop and the mall doesn't even close until seven. I've got all day to dedicate to this."

"I have grading to do, though," I protest.

"Correction: *future* Danielle has grading to do. *Present* Danielle gets to focus on herself." She hands off the dresses to the dressing room attendant, keeping only a glittery blue number that looked amazing on her.

It takes two iced coffees, one giant pretzel, and two more stores to find the dress. I don't know if I've ever spent that much time at the mall in my entire life, but I could not be happier with how I look in this dress. I am so excited to show it off to Charlie—he won't be able to keep his hands off me. Not to mention, it was on sale. Like, on sale *at the outlet store*. I guess not too many people are buying strapless dresses in the middle of winter.

Amanda convinces me that, since it's so late, we stop for dinner and drinks on the way back. We swing by one of those trendy places downtown and have a seat at the bar.

Not two sips into our drinks, her phone rings. She flips is over to see who is calling, and sends a quick text in response. "She will have to wait her turn. Sorry. What were you saying?"

"Yeah, no worries. I was just saying that it doesn't feel fair to Gabriel that his dad doesn't get to come to school events. Like, does he hate me for keeping his dad from going to the Christmas program?"

"It wasn't *you* keeping him from the program, it was his dad's own behavior. It is in no way your fault."

"But I could make it so his dad could be there just by talking to Mark."

She sighs, "It is totally up to you. I don't think you should, but I'm not the person who was basically assaulted by him."

My mind flashes to Adam taking the punch. "I guess Mr. Johnson should have a say, too. He's the one who—"

Amanda's phone rings again, interrupting us. She looks at the screen, first with annoyance, then concern.

"I'm going to take this, sorry."

I nod, taking a sip of my drink and turning away to give her some privacy. Little good it does, as the person on the other end is in near-hysterics. All I can make out is something along the lines of "I thought they were gone" being repeated over and over.

I flag down the bartender to see if they can cancel our food order. This sounded like something that might need immediate attention.

"Sweetie, you're going to be fine. I'm heading home now." She turns around, hand raised, but sees that I'm already talking to the bartender and goes back to her conversation. "We are leaving *right now*. I will be there soon."

I pay for our drinks and we are headed to the car, which isn't parked too far away.

"Is everything alright?" I ask as we half-run down the sidewalk.

"Yeah." Amanda shakes her head. "No. My girlfriend, she gets—" She stops in her tracks, looking at me with wide eyes. "I mean...my *roommate* gets seizures. It had been a long time since she's had one..."

I grab Amanda's hand and keep pushing forward to the car. "Are we headed to your place or the hospital?"

"My place."

"Good. I can drive so you can call or text your girlfriend if she needs you. I'll take a rideshare from your place after I'm sure you're both good." We arrive at the car and I hold out my hand for the keys.

Amanda smiles and rummages through her purse. "I'm sorry I didn't tell you. It's just...our job..." She holds her keys out.

I give as reassuring a grin as I can as I take them from her. "I understand completely. Charlie and I live together."

The entire drive, Amanda's face is illuminated by the glow of her cell phone. We forget to put on music, instead listening to the chimes of a steady stream of text messages and the clicks of the phone's keyboard.

I park in her driveway. "You want me to come in?"

Amanda shakes her head. "Bea gets really embarrassed when people see her anxious. You can meet her another time."

"I look forward to it. Now you go; I'll wait in the car. You text me when you're good and I'll request a ride. I'll leave your keys in the mailbox when I get picked up."

Amanda lets out a small sigh, the fog of her breath catching the cold air from the open car door. "Thanks."

She runs up to her door, nearly slipping on the icy cement steps.

I do puzzles on my phone until my battery hits 10%, the notification coming at the same moment as a text from Amanda telling me I am good to leave and thanking me again. I walk up the stairs, being cautious when I get to the slick one, and drop the keys in her letter box. There is calm music playing inside.

When I get home, Charlie is glued to his gaming chair and I completely forget to show him my dress. In fact, I only have enough energy to shower and pass out.

CHAPTER 10

The Valentine

Did you know that St. Valentine was beheaded? Fun fact, right? My teachers managed to gloss over that fact when I was in Catholic school, but I thought, *he's a Saint. We should celebrate him!* Then I found the truth on his Wikipedia page. I suppose I can gloss over it, too. I can't, however, avoid the "hammering nails through someone's hands and feet and then leaving him hanging there to die" that will be coming up just before Easter. *I'll have to ask Amanda how to approach that one...*

I'm running through the schedule for the day that I have written on the whiteboard. Class parties are best saved for the end of the day so the kids can be all sugared up right before they leave, but it's Friday, so the last part of the day is Reading Buddies...

"Want to do Valentine's Day together?" I hear a familiar voice ask from the doorway. I turn to see Adam in a pink shirt and red tie, his smile charming as ever.

I can't help but blush. "I...have plans." It's a lie, but he doesn't need to know that.

"I meant during the day. We can do cards in our own classes, then come together for cookies and juice or whatever instead of reading at the end of the day."

I look at the board. "That solves this problem, but I need to talk to someone about *The Fault in Our Stars*."

"Did you finish it?" he asks with hesitance in his voice.

"Not yet." I reach to switch the times for handwriting and math. The kids will be useless after lunch with an imminent party.

"What chapter are you on?"

I nod at my schedule. It will have to do. "Nineteen? I think. I just finished the chapter at the gas station."

He looks at me like I have two heads. "And you want to talk about *that* on Valentine's Day?"

"You're right. Maybe we should just eat a ridiculous amount of chocolate and call it a day."

"Then you can call me this weekend when you finish the book because..." he puffs out his cheeks, letting out a long breath.

"That bad?"

"I mean, I won't say that I cried—" he shrugs, "—but I might have cried."

I let out a small chuckle. "Yeah, I'll take a debrief, then."

He looks at the clock. "I have to go make copies before the class comes in, I'll see you at the end of the day!"

I look, too. *Shoot*. Five minutes until the bell and I haven't used the restroom yet. I rush out my door behind him and take the stairs two at a time. My kids are the last ones waiting outside when I finally make it to them, exaggerated shivering included.

I am in awe of how held-together my kids are. Not only is it Friday, but it is a holiday, *and* they will be getting candy and cookies. It is mind-blowing that we not only managed to get through everything

I had planned, but also have about half an hour to spare before the Reading Buddies come down.

"Since you were all so awesome today, what do you want to do with the free time?" I ask, not ready to try to throw together something educational.

"Can we make valentines for our buddies?" Ruth asks, playing with the ribbon on her box of cards from her classmates.

"Absolutely!" We break out the colored cardstock, glue sticks, scissors, stickers, and those little hole punchers that make shapes. I put on some "quiet working music," which is actually just LoFi versions of movie soundtracks. Today's pick: the Studio Ghibli playlist.

After I write some words on the board that they might want to use on their cards, Gabriel raises his hand, but doesn't wait for me to call on him to ask, "Miss Monroe, are you going to make one for your Reading Buddy?"

I start to laugh, but it is quickly drowned out by other kids agreeing with this idea.

"You should!"

"I think Mr. Johnson would like one!"

"I bet you make really pretty cards!"

It's been a while since I've done something crafty. Why not? I grab a few shades of red and pink and sit at the back table, cutting out polka dots. The task allows me to zone out, while obviously keeping an ear out for any commotion in the classroom. The kids, however, are equally focused on their own tasks, so my mind wanders to the intended recipient of this card. The feel of his coat on my bare shoulders. His musky, woodsy smell. That smile. How he makes me feel... safe. I only realize that I'm grinning like an infatuated schoolgirl when the principal pops in.

"Happy Valentine's Day, first grade!" he yells from the doorway, making me jump in my chair. I was a thousand percent zoned out.

The class cheerfully reciprocates and Principal Miller is none the wiser to my inattentiveness—or at least I hope that's the case.

As I'm adding the finishing touches to my card, Christine walks over to take a look.

She frowns down at it. "No hearts." It's not a question, just a sad observation.

"No, but I think the dots are kind of cute."

"It's not a valentine if it doesn't have hearts."

"Well, I say it still counts. Besides, Mr. Johnson is not my boyfriend. It might be strange to give him a card with hearts on it."

Christine raises one eyebrow at me. She's been practicing this move all year and I think her muscles finally have it down. "I gave a card with hearts to *Jeremy*, Miss Monroe, and he is definitely *not* my boyfriend."

I shake my head with a lighthearted chuckle and hold out my hand. "Hand me the stickers." I find a medium-sized heart sticker and adhere it to the bottom corner. "Better?"

She gives a huge grin, showing off her missing front tooth. "Much better."

We manage to clean up our scraps just in time to welcome the seventh graders. Each of my students rushes to their buddy once they enter the door and hand them a valentine with still-sticky glue, and the seventh grader hands them a card in return. Some of the older kids have looks of "I'm too cool for this" on their faces, but when they see their buddy's face light up upon receiving a card, it instantly softens.

The whole room is abuzz as the buddies work on coloring sheets and games, and the energy only increases as they eat cookies and drink juice.

I lean against the radiator. Sometimes it is too hot, but when I am wearing a skirt *and* leggings, it is just enough layers to make my hindquarters pleasantly warm, especially in contrast to the air that comes off the just-too-cold windows. Adam stands next to me, at first leaning against the radiator, too, but quickly backing off.

"Woah, yours is a lot warmer than mine."

"I suppose we're closer to the boiler down here. I think it's nice."

He reaches into his pants pocket and pulls out a purple card. A whole card. Curse men and their large pockets. "Happy Valentine's Day. My students said I should make one, too."

I hold out my finger. "Just a sec." I run to grab his off my desk. "My kids told me the same."

"Oooooooh!" A young man's voice rings out as if it was some scandal.

"Oh, shut it, Brady!" Adam says playfully. "You're the one who suggested I make one."

"Yeah, but she made one for you, too!" Addison chimes in.

"You should ask her out!" another seventh grader adds.

Adam shifts to that face that every teacher has in their back pocket for when things are getting a bit too rowdy. "She has a boyfriend. Now, will you please enjoy your party with your buddies?"

They look away, but I keep my eyes on his face. *Is that really the only thing keeping him from asking me out?*

When he turns back, I look away, but not quickly enough. The moment of eye contact sends my heart racing. When my cheeks begin to blush, I turn toward the window, leaning onto the ledge and letting the cold late winter chill cool my face, hoping he hadn't noticed. *You are being an idiot. The holiday is messing with your head.*

After a few breaths I feel more myself and turn around to find Adam watching me. "Wow, this radiator *is* pretty warm today." I fan myself, hoping to explain away the remaining flush to my cheeks.

He blinks twice before shaking his head. "Ready for the weekend?" It wasn't so much a question, more of a check-in.

My chest heaves under a deep sigh. "Very, but I think a cookie might help me survive the last few minutes. Want one?"

He thinks for a second then says, "Nah, I'll probably take one to-go after, though."

I snag a frosted cookie from the undisturbed part of the pack—the part I know no kids' hands have been all over just yet. Even with the "take the first one you touch" rule, they still manage to bump and nudge three or four others while taking their one cookie out.

With my mouth half-full of pink frosting, I ask, "Any plans for tonight?"

A hint of excitement flashes across his face, but leaves all too suddenly. "No. Maybe watch some terrible rom-com just to say I did."

What was that momentary emotion? Had he had plans that he, for that brief instant, forgot had fallen through?

I shrug. "Same, probably."

He pushes himself off the wall, standing up straighter. "Are you and your boyfriend not...?"

There it is. Time for the conversation I hate. "Nah, Charlie doesn't like Valentine's Day. He thinks it's some scheme to sell candy and cards." I leave out the part about it formerly being one of my favorite holidays. "I guess it's fine. It means we don't have to fight other people for dinner reservations and I usually just buy myself discount candy on the 15th."

He gives a sympathetic smile. "Well, this year you'll need that candy when you finish *The Fault in our Stars*. Then you can text me when you need the emotional support."

I pull out my phone, ready to get his number, then pause when I see a text from Charlie. It's nothing special, just asking about where I put something, but it reminds me that this schoolyard crush is nothing but that. I turn the screen back off. "How about we just discuss it next week? I can use the time to decompress and we can have a proper talk about the whole book."

He nods in understanding, but his brow has a slight crease of disappointment. Maybe he just *really* wants to talk about that book with someone.

After school, I get home and drop my bag under the coat rack. A purple paper peeks out of the top and I reach for it, realizing I never actually opened it during the chaos of the party. Across the front it said "Happy Valentine's Day" and the inside read "I lucked out with my Reading Buddy assignment. – Adam."

The handwriting is legible at best, and the cutting and gluing looked like it might have been done by a primary student, but my heart warmed at the effort he went through to make it—and the fact he *did* make it, even if it was only with the encouragement of his class.

"Did one of your students ask you to be their valentine?" Charlie asks from his computer. He is still in his flannel sweats and a white tank top.

"No, this is from another teacher," I respond, not looking away from the card.

"Well, tell him hands off. You're taken." He throws a handful of trail mix into his mouth and goes back to typing something.

The stark contrast between the card and those words hits me. I can't say it was the first time I considered how different things could be if I weren't with Charlie, but everyone has those thoughts from time to time in a relationship, right? We've been together for years, and I know exactly how green this grass is. Why even entertain the idea of the other side?

I head to our room and open my laptop, scanning Netflix for some Hallmark-style movies: those incredibly fictional narratives that never *actually* happen. I turn one on and settle in for the night.

Monday morning, I find on my desk a box of chocolates—rectangle, not a heart—with three black pom poms sitting on top. I read the post-it:

> Danielle,
> I hope the cheesy rom-com you watched was better than the one I ended up watching. I walked by the discount chocolate on Saturday and thought you might need more. Also, nice choice in playlist on Friday.
> — Adam

I set the note down and pick up one of the puffs. It is made of black yarn and has googly eyes attached. A smile grows across my face. Songs from Totoro were on the Studio Ghibli playlist. He made me soot sprites.

CHAPTER 11

The Hike

I t is finally one of those late-winter days when it isn't absolutely miserable outside. Better yet, it isn't raining, and it wasn't raining yesterday, so the ground isn't littered with puddles. Best of all, it's Saturday, so Amanda and I plan to meet for a walk. We'd done this once or twice in the fall, but only around school and the conversations were mostly school-related. I feel like our relationship has grown since then.

I am thrilled to pick her up because this is the first time I get to see her house. Even more because her girlfriend Bea is home. In fact, she is the one who opens the door.

She greets me with a warm smile. "You must be Dani. Come on in. Amanda is taking her time getting ready, as usual." She steps out of the doorway to let me in, her tight curls bouncing with each step.

Amanda comes around the corner, pulling her long hair back into a tight ponytail. She is in full athletic gear, in contrast to my coziest flannel sweats.

"Oh, so we're *hiking* hiking," I note.

Bea chuckles. "She would wear those leggings every day if I let her. For all I know, she's dressed for a coffee date."

Amanda scurries over to drop a peck on Bea's cheek. "Which reminds me—text me your coffee order. We'll pick it up on the way home."

Bea's hands shoot to her phone. "Can I get the ridiculously over-the-top one?"

Amanda squints her eyes, considering. "Yes. Only because I love you."

The exchange tugs my heart in multiple directions: warmed by the sentiment, saddened by the fact they have to hide, and haunted by a twinge of... envy?

No. Just because a relationship is different, it doesn't mean it's better. Just because it has aspects you admire doesn't mean what you have isn't worth keeping.

We're half a mile into a trail at Marquam Nature Park when these thoughts finally boil over. "How long have you and Bea been together?"

She looks up, doing some mental math. "Two years? Three if you count from our first date, but she didn't want to put a title on it until I was ready to come out to my family."

"So your family knows?" I am so focused on Amanda that I nearly trip on a tree root.

"Oh yeah. And most of them took it well. My mom had to help my dad come around, but it didn't take long. My dad's parents won't speak to me—but I think that has to do more with me dating someone who is black than dating a woman."

"Oh, shit."

"Yeah, we didn't talk to them much before I came out, so no great loss for us. They wouldn't have been invited to the wedding, anyways."

I stop in my tracks. "The wedding?"

Amanda grabs my arm and pulls me along. "No. Not yet. I mean, we've talked about it and we know it's in the cards, but we have some stuff to figure out first."

"Like how the school will take it?"

She gives a wide-eyed, desperate smile. "Exactly. As long as I'm not married, there's some plausible deniability for Mark. He can claim he knows nothing about me or my love life. But once she's on my taxes? The archdiocese might step in and say something."

I freeze again, oblivious to the power-walkers behind us who barely stop in time to not run into me. "Oh, sorry... Does Principal Miller know?"

"You can't keep stopping. I need momentum to keep going." She yanks my arm again. "And yes, Mark knows. He mentioned seeing me at a restaurant with my *friend*—emphasis and everything—then told me that if a few key parents from the school saw what he saw, they could cause trouble for me. Apparently, he caught the goodbye kiss." She shakes off the memory. "But enough about me, what about you and Charlie? Remind me—how long have you been together?"

"Five years next week."

"Five years? You think he'll propose soon?"

"No. He... doesn't believe in marriage."

"Oh." The word is more disappointed than surprised. "But if you have kids, you'll need to be married first to keep your job."

"I'm not sure I'll be sticking with Catholic schools for long. Besides, Charlie doesn't want kids."

This time, Amanda stops, but she is smart enough to tuck herself to the side of the trail. "But what do *you* want?"

Something shatters in my chest. I never felt too strongly one way or the other about having kids, but while teaching I found that I love being around children, and that kids make my life more fun. There *has* been a growing desire to have my own, but I've been pushing it down every time I've felt it.

Before I know it, I'm crying. Full-on bawling. My words are barely comprehensible over my lungs' desperate attempts to refill themselves. "I don't know what I want." I know Amanda was only asking about kids and marriage, but the question resonated further into the recesses of my life. *What do I want?* That was never the question I asked myself. It was always framed as *What can I have while making Charlie happy?* Because making Charlie happy *does* make me happy, but what *else* could bring me joy? Bring me fulfillment? Bring me passion?

Amanda is rubbing my back as I am snotting all over the sleeve of my sweatshirt. Other groups pass us by, but I don't dare look up. Wrinkled hands hold a tissue to my face. I let out a whispered "thank you" and take it, forcing a smile at the old lady before she goes.

"I think you and Charlie might have some stuff to talk out."

I let out a deep, though stuttered, breath. "Yeah, we might."

We change topics, discussing our plans for the Seattle trip and the wedding. We have two nights booked at a hotel downtown, not far from the stop for the shuttle that will take us to the venue. Our list of things to do in town before the wedding keeps growing: watch the people throwing the fish, go up the Space Needle, go on a boat tour—anything overly touristy that we can fit into one day, we're doing it.

When I get home, I am sipping my over-the-top iced coffee. The one that Bea ordered just sounded too good to pass up.

"Do you need that much sugar?" Charlie teases from his desk. His headphones are swaying on their stand—he was just playing video games, despite his manuscript being pulled up on his screen. Why does he feel the need to hide his gaming on a weekend?

"It was a long hike and I deserve it." I smile as if the hike was the greatest accomplishment in the world. I feel so good after that cry.

"Don't forget we're supposed to be cutting back on spending." He turns back to his keyboard and taps out a word or two, then leans back.

I deserve to treat myself with the money I earn, I think to myself. *I could tell him that, but then it would start a fight. I'm just not feeling a fight today.* I think back to the conversation on the trail. "Hey, can we talk?"

He lets out a long sigh, then closes his document. "Fine. What's up?"

"I was wondering if we could revisit the idea of having kids." I see the expression on his face change and backpedal a bit. "I mean, just check in and see if we're still on the same page."

"What? Are you thinking you want kids now?" He scoffs.

"I don't know." I shrug. Something inside me squashes down the desire. "Maybe."

"Are you ovulating right now? Your hormones are probably telling you that you want kids. Wait a week and you'll change your mind."

"I'm on the pill. I don't ovulate."

"Well, I'm not having kids. Ever. So find joy in having all your students to care for and no diapers to change." He turns away from me and opens his video game. The icon on the home menu shows he's logged over 500 hours on it.

Didn't he just get this for Christmas? It's March. I do some mental math. If he spent 10 hours every weekend day playing, about twelve weeks since Christmas, that would be about 240 hours. Add ten hours a week for a few hours every night... that's around 350 hours... *When is he finding the time to play this game?* I snap back to the conversation. "Okay. No kids. Just wanted to see where we stood."

Why did I think he was going to have a sudden change of heart? I knew what I signed up for when I started dating him: no marriage, no kids. I should be happy with what I have, with what we've built over the past five years. I am lucky to have someone who has stayed with me through grad school, through job hunting. I should be happy, right?

...right?

CHAPTER 12

The Change in Plans

T-minus two hours until Spring Break. Err... Easter Break. The days off are always the week after Easter here.

Since it's Holy Week, our calendars have been filled with Masses, assemblies, and Stations of the Cross. It's amazing how unfazed six- and seven-year-olds are by the story of a guy getting brutally executed... or maybe they just weren't paying attention. Likely the latter with a hint of "I blame violent video games."

But today is Good Friday—a somber day remembering the crucifixion and death of Jesus. In fact, dismissal today is supposed to be silent. *Silent.* Have you ever tried to make over a dozen first graders be silent? As they're leaving school? On a half day? At the start of a week off?

I'm in the middle of giving a math test when Amanda appears at my door. Keeping half my focus on my class, I mouth, "What?"

She gestures for me to come over and I pay closer attention to her face. Her expression is frantic, almost crazed. She is picking at the backpack strap slung over her shoulder.

I step away from Nicolette. "Just work on the ones you can, sweetie. I'll be back to read the word problems in a bit." I hurry to the door. "Are you okay? Who is with your students?"

Given the look on her face, her voice is surprisingly hollow. "Mrs. Smith has them. It's Bea. She fell."

I bring my voice low. "Oh my God. Is she okay? Was it a seizure?"

"They think so. She hit her head really bad. One of her coworkers found her unconscious..." It sounds like there is more to say, but if she continued with the thought she would have lost her composure. She shakes whatever image was haunting her from her mind. "I am on my way to the hospital. I am so sorry, I don't think I'll be able to go to the wedding with you."

"Don't worry about that. Go! Keep me posted on how she's doing." I turn to see my class all focused on their papers, heads tucked into their privacy folders, and pull Amanda in for a hug. She is shaking. *Shit. It must be really bad...* "Alice and I will make sure your kids get to their parents at dismissal."

Amanda squeezes me hard. "I am so sorry."

"Don't be. I'll figure it out. Go." I pull away, half-shoving her in the direction of the front door.

I am shocked at my students. Nicolette still hasn't even come to get me. She usually needs me to walk her through each problem twice, but she seems to have packed some independence in her backpack today. I run to my phone and send Charlie a message.

Danielle: I NEED the car this weekend.

I don't have time to check my phone for the rest of the day. Silent dismissal was more successful than expected, but Jeremy used the silence as his cue to be his loudest. No words—just harrumphs, groans, giggles, and an over-dramatic "OW!" when someone lightly nudged him in line. Now, I see messages from the two people I wanted to hear from: Amanda and Charlie. I check Amanda's first.

> Amanda: Bea is awake and talking. Apparently, she hit the corner of something on her way down so there was a lot of blood.
> Amanda: They're going to keep her here through the weekend to make sure there's no swelling or major damage.
> Amanda: I am so sorry for having to bail on you.

I breathe a sigh of relief. My stomach had been in a knot having Bea in the back of my mind.

> Danielle: Please stop apologizing. You take care of your lady.
> Danielle: Let me know when you two get home. I'd be happy to drop off a dinner or something when I'm back from the wedding.

I open the messages from Charlie.

> Charlie: no can do. i'm going to Matt's cabin with the guys.
> Charlie: what? your friend doesnt want to go with you anymore?

I fume. So much for responsibilities at home that he has to take care of... I start to text out a response but decide a call would be easier.

It rings three times before he picks up.

"Some friend bailing on you last minute." I can hear the hum of the road as he yells over speakerphone.

I try to keep my voice low, knowing some of the other teachers in the building are doing three hours of silence in remembrance of the death of Jesus. "She had an emergency come up. Her friend is in the hospital."

"Oh, shit. Sorry. But yeah, you can't take the car. I'm already halfway to Craig's house to pick him up."

He wasn't even going to say goodbye? "Then how am I supposed to get to Seattle?"

"I don't know, take the train maybe? It drops you off basically downtown."

"Alright. Let me check something." I pull up the train schedule on my computer. There is one leaving in 20 minutes—not helpful—and another leaving at 7:30 tonight that will get me in around...eleven. "It gets me kind of close to the hotel, this says it's a 20-minute walk, but I'm not sure I want to be getting off a train in a strange city at nearly midnight by myself."

There is silence on his end for a bit. "I'm not sure I want you doing that, either. Why don't you just stay home, huh?"

I consider it. A weekend at home, alone. It does sound nice, and if Amanda and Bea need anything I could just swing by and... Nope. Not without the car. I would be *trapped* at home all weekend. "Because I want to go to this wedding. I want to see Carl and Anthony get married. I want to stay in the hotel room I've already paid for." Something inside me snaps. "You know what? Speaking of paying for stuff, who paid the registration on that car? And who pays for the insurance? Me. I should get more of a say in whether or not I get to use the car I pay for." I realize a beat too late that I also paid for the gas that he was currently using, but I didn't want to add anything that would break the tension he was hopefully feeling on his end.

"Too bad. I'm using the car already."

"Then help me find a safe way to get to Seattle tonight!" I am pacing the room at this point, but upon the next turn, I see a figure in my doorway. My heart jumps in surprise. It is at this moment I realize that I had been basically screaming.

Adam points at me, then does a thumbs-up with a questioning face. A "you good?" without any words.

My face contorts as I feel like I'm about to cry. "Whatever. I'll figure it out," I say to Charlie, barely keeping my composure, before I end the call. I look at Adam and shake my head.

In three long strides, he has me in an embrace. My face is buried in his shirt and I take in the woodsy smell that I've come to look forward to whenever he is nearby. I am surprised by how much anger I had bottled up, but Adam allows me time to cry it out. He says nothing, just holds me. When my breathing goes back to normal, he pulls away, cupping my cheeks with his hands. He bends lower, giving me a half-smile as he glances down at my lips, then gazes back into my eyes. I have the urge to lean forward and kiss him but hold back to see where he thinks this is going. He takes his thumbs and rubs the last of the tears off of my cheeks before he turns away, bee-lining for a stack of papers.

I nearly fall forward, but a quick step saves me. Maybe I had been subconsciously trying to lean in.

Adam comes back with a piece of lined paper and a pen, then scribbles out a note.

He's doing the three hours of silence. I kick myself. *He wasn't trying to kiss me, he was trying to show me he cared or that he was sorry without using words.* Well, thank goodness I didn't try to kiss him...

He slaps the paper down in front of me. It reads: "I am spending Easter with my folks just north of Seattle. I wasn't going to leave until tomorrow morning, but they'd be happy to have me a day early if you want to drive up with me."

I look at him, eyes wide and mouth agape. "Are you serious?!" This time I wrap my arms around him, going on my tiptoes to hold around his neck. "This is amazing. Thank you so much!"

When I finally let him go, he goes back to the paper and writes: "I want to get there before it's too dark, so leave around 2? Then we only have to drive in silence for an hour before I can bore you with my thoughts on books. I'm going to run home and finish packing."

It is 12:30 now and my bag is already packed and stuffed behind my desk. It feels weird to have a one-sided conversation, so I take the pen and write: "Sure. I'll just hang out here and put some grades in until you're ready to go."

Sitting at my desk, doing mindless data entry, I find my train of thought constantly wandering back to Charlie. Charlie and his friends. Charlie deciding to spend the weekend at the cabin without even telling me. I'm mad at him. I've *been* mad at him, even if I've never acknowledged it. But how long have I felt like this? How long have we both been prioritizing *him*? And why was a glance at my lips all it took for me to want to throw away what Charlie and I have?

CHAPTER 13

The Road Trip

One hour of complete silence. It was fine while I looked around Portland. The mountains were out, so I made sure to admire them. The river was beautiful. Once we made it through Vancouver, though, the views were not as interesting.

I let my mind wander again, but this time made sure to *not* think about Charlie. I didn't want to spend this trip being upset. I wanted to be happy and celebratory, even if I was going to be alone. I think back to my time in college, nights out with Carl and his friends. I wonder who will all be there. I think of the people I look forward to seeing, as well as the people I hope can't make it. The purposeful contemplation becomes peaceful, almost like a meditation of me willing a fun weekend into existence.

Somewhere near a town called Longview, I am startled when the silence is suddenly broken by Adam's voice. "And that's time."

When I say I jump, that is an incredible understatement. We could have been about to get in a car wreck and I don't think I would have been nearly as startled. I have one hand on the handle above the door and the other clutching the center console. My entire ass is out of the seat for a good second or two before my body finally releases the tension.

Adam is laughing. Hard.

When I finally regain control of my limbs, I swat at him with the back of my hand. "You could have warned me."

He is still laughing through his words. "Wouldn't that require talking?"

"Shut up."

"I was just quiet for three hours. I am not shutting up." He hands me his phone, unlocked. "Choose something." Just before I grab it, he pulls it away. "Something *not* from the Twilight soundtrack."

I reach over and take it from him. "No promises." I browse for a while, not knowing what kind of music might be the right vibe for the trip, then ask, "Are we going to be talking over it or no? Because I need to know if I need to choose sing-along music."

"Well that depends on how good of a singer you are..." He gives me a sidelong glance.

"Instrumental it is, then!" I pop on a playlist of Nintendo soundtracks—you know, Mario, Zelda, Pokemon.

"A fan of the classics, I see. Now tell me more about this wedding you're going to."

How does he know about the—Oh, right. He overheard my conversation with Charlie... not hard to overhear someone yelling, I guess. "Just an old friend from college—undergrad, not teacher prep. He's getting married at Brackhill Manor."

Adam whistles. "Swanky. But that's on the other side of the water, shouldn't you be staying in Bellevue or something?"

"They hired a shuttle that will pick us up in Downtown Seattle and bring us over and back." I catch myself. "Not us, me. It was supposed to be me and Amanda going, but her roommate is in the hospital so I am all by myself."

"I'd be happy to stand in as your dance partner."

A smile spreads across my face as I think about dancing with Adam. I can imagine his arms around me, looking up at his face—not too drastically due to the fact I have impossibly high heels to wear, and swaying to some Ed Sheeran song. He would look down at me and give his half-smirk, but when I smile back at him, the huge grin comes out. We would lean in closer, and... *Nope. Not entertaining this thought.* "Nah, I think I'll be alright flying solo. Carl and I had a lot of the same friends in college, so I will know plenty of people there."

"My mom would probably prefer me staying home to help her prep for Easter breakfast, anyways. Though, I would love to see what you would wear to a wedding at Brackhill."

"I'll be sure to send you a picture once I get ready."

"Then you'll probably need my number. Also, I want you to have it in case you get stuck somewhere. I'm only twenty minutes out of the city in good traffic, so if you need rescuing I will be able to swing down."

I pull out my phone, thumbs hovering over it in feigned suspense until he starts listing off his digits. "I'll send you a text so you have mine, too. I'll make it very clear who it is." I input three book emojis and hit send.

"It was all emojis, wasn't it?" he asks.

"Yeah," I admit. "But which ones?"

He narrows his eyes. "A vampire, a wolf, and a shrug."

"Wrong. But I think I like that better than what I did."

"You know, my cousin was telling me about a book that is just like *Twilight*. Maybe we should give it a go."

My eyes go wide. "You're kidding."

"Apparently it's what the kids are reading these days. I've seen at least three of my students with it. At the very least, it can't be *worse* than *Twilight*."

I bite my lip, wincing. "What is it called?"

"*Crave*." He stretches the word out, trying to make it sound interesting.

"I'm going to pass, but you go ahead and tell me how it is."

"Maybe I'll get the audiobook and make you start it with me on the drive back to Portland."

"You're giving me a ride home, too?"

"I don't see why not. My family likes to do Easter at the cathedral, so we can pick you up while we're down there, you come up for some Easter breakfast, then we drive back down once the day's festivities are over."

It does sound like a lot of fun. My family was never big on Easter. "I don't want to impose..."

"Not an imposition at all. My mom always makes plenty of extra food and I bet one of my nieces would love to have you as a partner in the egg hunt."

I sit up a little straighter. Maybe I did end up willing a fun weekend into existence. "Sure. That sounds fun."

We spend the rest of the drive discussing books we've read—both solo and as buddies.

CHAPTER 14

The Ceremony

The shuttle picks me up at five, along with a dozen other people waiting at our stop. It's not quite a shuttle, though–more like the lovechild of a limo and a party bus. I see one person I recognize–Elena, she was in a few of my classes in college. We sit together for the 30-minute drive in plush seats.

We drive over one of two parallel floating bridges. One side has choppy water while the other seems completely flat, and the banks are a rich green dotted with large houses. A beautiful skyline can be seen in front of us, and another behind us.

Elena leans in close and points down the far bank. "That's Bill Gates' neighborhood. And Anthony's parents live just a little bit south." She gives me an eyebrow raise.

"Damn. So they're, like, *rich*." My voice drops for the last word.

"Private yacht rich," Elena adds.

Is it tacky to be talking about someone else's wealth? I mean, someone you sort of know? *Nah...* And if it is, I don't care. Carl would appreciate me getting up to date on all the gossip.

We drive through a city called Bellevue, then venture further out into the mountains. After a random exit, a winding road, and an incredibly long driveway, we come upon a freaking *mansion*. The looped drive is full of town cars, with torches lighting the path. Replace the vehicles with carriages and I'd swear we were arriving for a ball at... that place the guy from Pride and Prejudice is from... Pem-something... Anyways...

We pull up to the front and a man in black tie is helping us down the stairs of the bus, which is good because these heels are dangerous. The air still has an early spring chill to it, but the warmth of the torches keeps us comfortable enough as we make our way to the house.

As we step inside, my growing suspense and excitement are suddenly squashed. The first face I see is him. *Him.* Nate. Nathan Jones. I had successfully pushed him from my mind for the past half-decade, but now there is no avoiding him, because he's seen me, too. I turn to cling to Elena, but she already walked off to talk to other friends. *Shit, shit, shit.*

"You came alone?" Nate's greasy smile spreads across his face as the smell of his body spray comes in range.

"Hi, Nate." I try to be cordial, but dismissive.

Apparently, he picks up on the former but not the latter. His eyes scan me up and down. "The one that got away." He draws out both his gaze and his words.

I give him a pressed-lip smile that verges on a snarl. "The one who was never interested, Nate. Please, go bother someone else."

"And leave you all alone? I'd never." He reaches for my arm.

Apparently calling the cops on a guy for harassment and trespassing wasn't enough of a hint. I could threaten to call again, but I would never make a threat I wouldn't follow through with—and there's no way I'm going to involve the cops during my friend's super bougie wedding.

So, Nate won't honor my feelings, but he might honor another guy's...

"I'm not sure my boyfriend would appreciate me hanging around another guy tonight."

Nate leans in close, his arm reaching around my shoulders, and whispers, "Well, I don't see your boyfriend here, now do I?" My skin crawls when his lips touch my cheek.

I shove him away as hard as I can, nearly losing my balance and drawing stares from partygoers nearby. "He is on his way. Leave me alone."

He stands in shocked silence as I rush to another room and close the door behind me.

A catering waitress starts saying, "You can't be here yet, we're still setting–" before she sees my face and changes her tune. "Take your time, sweetheart."

I pull out my phone from my handbag. No way Charlie would come up here–even if he did, it wouldn't be for over four hours. I think back to the serious Mr. Costa vibes that Nate was giving off. If I just had someone that would place themself between me and him...

> Danielle: Someone here is making me really uncomfortable. Any chance you have something formal to wear?

I slide down the wall, coming to rest on the ground. My eyes are locked on my phone. He hasn't even read it yet. Of course. He is with his family; he might not even have his phone with him. It's foolish of me to even think he would drop everything and come to my rescue for the second time this weekend.

The waitress approaches me gently. "I'm sorry to interrupt, ma'am, but the ceremony is going to start in a few minutes. You may want to go find a seat."

I thank her and gather my courage. My phone buzzes in my hand.

Cherry: Heads up: Nate is here.

Cherry was there the night I called the cops. She is one of the few people who knows what happened the night that he wouldn't leave my apartment. She is the one who stayed to make sure I wouldn't be alone with him.

Danielle: I know. Hiding from him now. Save a spot
for me if you can?

I silence my phone, straighten my dress, and walk out of the room. The main foyer is basically empty save for a few ushers collecting stragglers. No Nate in sight. *Phew.*

When I get to the ceremony space, I am waved down by Cherry, who then indicates the space next to her. I shimmy across a few people who are already seated and embrace Cherry.

"I thought you were still in Beijing!" She had moved home after college, rarely ever coming back to the States due to a fear of flying.

"I have a job interview in New York next week, so I am having an extended layover on my way there. I didn't even know I was coming until a few days ago." She rubbed my arm. "You look great, by the way."

I gesture back to her. "Look who's talking–you look amazing!"

The violin that has been playing is joined by the rest of a string quartet and we settle into our seats. The setting is gorgeous. We are outside, but there is a lattice awning supporting heat lamps that are set to *just* the right temperature to not need a second layer. Patio lights are draped over the seating, but the wedding arch gets its own spotlights. There are white roses everywhere, accented with the green of the stems and leaves.

The parents enter first, followed by the wedding party, all with forest green dresses and accent pieces. I see a lot of college acquaintances in this group.

Finally, the grooms walk in together, dressed in black tuxedos with green accents, arm in arm. Carl can't take his eyes off Anthony, and every time Anthony glances over to him, he beams, too. They are so in love and everyone here gets to witness as they promise each other forever.

The ceremony is beautiful. I cry, I laugh, and I cry some more. Cherry hands me a tissue at one point because apparently my mascara is starting to run. I can't help it, though. This is so beautiful. Their parents are glowing with pride. A stab shoots through my heart when I remember my mom will never see me get married. I look around at the guests, all filled with joy and excitement for the love this couple shares. Another pang of emotion—*Nobody* will ever see me get married.

"I now present, for the first time as spouses, Carl and Anthony!"

Guests throw confetti as the couple walks back up the aisle, Carl picking some out of Anthony's hair every few steps.

The wedding party disappears, I assume for pictures, while we are all left to mingle at a cocktail hour that spans multiple rooms on the first floor. I'm excited to get to do some exploring, but first, a drink is in order. As Cherry runs to use the restroom, I hop in line for one of the open bars. I reach into my purse to check my phone when I am interrupted by a tap on my shoulder.

"You can't be done alrea—" I turn to see... not Cherry.

"Your boyfriend get lost or something?" Nate is slurring his words. When did he have time to drink between the ceremony and now? Unless he was drinking during...

"I was just about to text him to check in." I am too nervous to add venom to my voice. He is uncomfortably close.

He narrows his eyes. "I think you're just trying to put me off."

He called my bluff. Shit. I wrap my fingers around my phone in my bag. "You know what? I think I'll call him. I don't want him texting and driving. If you'll excuse me." I push past him, giving up my spot in line. A shame, too, because I was third from the front. I make my way through the rooms with purpose, finding a route to the front door to get some fresh air.

The cold air of dusk hits my face as I leave the building. I take a lungful, only realizing as I exhale that I am shaking. Should I just leave?

I take out my phone to tell Cherry where I went, but I see a message notification from a while ago.

Adam: I'll be there as soon as I can.

Just knowing he is on his way sends a wave of relief through me. I think I can face it now. I turn to go back inside but hear the crunch of quick steps on gravel behind me.

"Excuse me, do you think you could help me find my Reading Buddy?"

CHAPTER 15

The Cocktail Hour

I literally just saw him yesterday, but my whole body warms with joy when I turn around and see his face. Everything about his presence here brings me joy. The way his suit fits, how the torchlight shadows dance across his face, the warmth in his voice. It all takes my breath away.

"Thank God you're here," I whisper under my breath as I rush to hug him.

His body is stiff at first, then slowly melts as his arms wrap around me. He holds me in silence for a few seconds before he takes his chin down to bring his lips close to my ear. "Are you okay?" The warmth of his breath sends a tingle down my spine.

I push my head into his chest just a touch further. "I think so." His scent is still there, buried deep under a stale closet smell. I take a step back, gesturing to his apparel. "Just had this lying around?"

He adjusts his sleeves by the cuff, then straightens his tie. "Well, it was intended for another wedding that never happened, so I'm glad I finally get to use it."

A wedding that never happened?

He must see the confusion on my face, because he holds up his left hand, showing me the palm and the back while shrugging.

He really was on the brink of marrying that girl. "Oh, wow. I'm sorry."

"It sucked, but preferable to finding everything out after the wedding. Speaking of weddings—" he holds out his arm for me to take, "—I think we have somewhere to be."

I take it gladly. Walking in the second time is ten times more magical. The cocktail hour is in full swing and the warm lighting against the dark windows makes the giant room feel cozy. Best of all, when I see Nate this time, he takes one glance at Adam and looks away. Something tells me it's not the last I'll see of him tonight, but at least he will not ruin this moment.

"Is that the person?" Adam's voice is loud enough for me to hear, but hushed enough to be lost to those around us.

"Is it really that obvious that he's a creep? You can tell just by looking at him?" I couldn't tell back then. What a great superpower.

"I can tell by how you look like you're trying to kill him with your eyes."

Yep, apparently I've been staring at him this whole time. Always keep an eye out for predators, I suppose—animal instincts kicking in. I break my death glare and look up at my date. "Can I buy you a drink?"

After I order two beers, Adam also asks the bartender for two shots of vodka. "One for each of us—we need to catch up with everyone else." He gestures to the crowd of guests, all clearly taking advantage of the free booze. His glass held in the air, he says, "To having the best Reading Buddy."

I hold back a ridiculous grin and repeat his words. "To having the best Reading Buddy." I down the shot and try my best not to make a face, but fail miserably. My eyes go so wide they threaten to pop out of their sockets while my mouth contorts. Adam almost spits out his shot when he sees my face, causing me to cough-laugh with the lingering alcohol vapors in my throat. That makes him laugh even harder, the shot still precariously in his mouth. The mix of pain and humor on his face proceeds to make me nearly lose it.

Adam finally turns around so he can compose himself without me messing it up.

"Holy cow, Dani. Try to kill me, why don't you?"

I'm still holding back a light cough. "Me? You're the one who lost it. I can't help if I make a face."

"You are welcome to make a face, but does it have to be *that* face?"

I pick up our beers and thank the bartender, nudging Adam, who is grabbing a handful of bar mix from the counter, out of the way. "It wasn't *that* bad."

Adam stops, faces me, and copies my face. Yeah, I guess it *was* that bad.

"Fine, it was my fault." I hand him his beer. "Rinse your poor mouth out."

I watch the bottle as he brings it to his soft lips. He is shaking his head, his smile wide, as he looks to the ceiling. When he finishes his sip, his eyes fall onto mine. He glances at my mouth then lets out a smug laugh.

I try to register what just happened when I feel my dry canine tooth snag on my lip. *Why is it dry? Why is it on my lip? Oh, shit...* In true Bella Swan fashion, I had been biting my lip the entire time I was watching him. "Sorry, I just spaced out for a second."

"Yeah, okay." The amusement in Adam's voice is palpable.

Perfect time to change the subject. "Shall we explore?"

He holds out his arm and I take it, sipping my beer so I can blame the blush on the alcohol. We make our way through some rooms, checking out how the other half lives. I mostly notice the major details, but Adam points out little intricacies that I don't quite catch—the leaves on the crown moulding, the color coordination of the books in the library, even the family crest that appears in each room.

When the emcee makes the announcement, the party makes its way to the dining tables. I do a lap around ours, checking the place cards. I let out a little "Yoink!" as I pull Nate's card from the spot across from me, trading him out for a random woman at the next table over—Eunice. Eunice sounds like she would be better company than Nate. I give an apology under my breath for the others at his new table.

Adam and I are the first to be seated, and Cherry soon joins us. "Where have you been? I was looking all over—" She stops as she sees Adam. "Oh, hello." She tucks her hair behind her ear as her eyelashes flutter.

A wave of jealousy comes over me before I realize I have no right to feel possessive of him. "Oh, Cherry, this is my..." I look at Adam. Do I say date? Coworker? Reading Buddy?

"Plus one." Adam stands and offers his hand. "Adam. Pleasure to meet you, Cherry."

"Pleasure is all mine." They sit, and it takes a beat for Cherry's gaze to switch back to me. She mouths one word: "boyfriend?"

I shake my head quickly, my eyes wide.

"Oh, you make it seem like it would be a bad thing," Adam cuts in.

Cherry covers her laugh with her hand.

"I mean, no, but..." I bring my head closer to them, implying a secret. "If Nate asks, then Adam is my boyfriend. It was the only way

I could think of to keep him from being a creep. My actual boyfriend was busy this weekend."

Cherry nods in understanding as more people join our table, including Elena. It's quite a fun group from college, plus Eunice, an eighty-something-year-old friend of Anthony's grandmother who just downed a glass of white wine like it was water.

Adam leans toward me. "Have you told your actual boyfriend that I'm here?"

I fiddle with my name card, feeling to see if the writing was from a printer or calligraphy. It's the latter—super fancy. "No. He's at a cabin in the middle of nowhere, so calls don't go through and texts are spotty."

"I'd like it if you texted him anyway. Just let him know." He pulls away, his focus going back to Cherry, who is asking him questions.

I pull out my phone. It's a simple request, and the tone in his voice implied it really was important to him, so I oblige.

> Danielle: Hey Charlie, my coworker Adam who gave
> me a ride to Seattle is at the wedding as my plus one.

I put my phone away and look up to see that Eunice is on a lengthy rant about how she used to know many gay men in her youth and how glad she is that they are allowed to get married now. Adam glances over at me questioningly.

Shit. Shit shit shit. How did I invite my Catholic coworker to a gay wedding without doing a vibe check first *twice*? I let a sheepish grin creep across my face and whisper, "Carl and Anthony."

He pauses for a moment, buffering, until his confusion melts. "Old lady's story now makes a lot more sense. I was trying to figure out if she was senile."

I laugh, almost too loud. "I suppose context was important there."

A string quartet version of "Marry You" by Bruno Mars starts playing over the speakers. The wedding party dances their way in, with Carl and Anthony raising their held hands at the end of the procession. Everyone stands and the room explodes with applause. I could feel the joy radiating from everyone there—from the couple themselves, from their proud parents, from every person celebrating with them. I look up at Adam, who has a huge grin on his face as he claps for the couple he had never even seen before until just now.

The music shifts to "Truly Madly Deeply" as the couple stets foot on the dance floor. I have high expectations for this first dance, as Carl is the type of person to learn the choreography to anything and everything. I am not as sure about Anthony, but I am almost positive Carl would never marry anybody with two left feet.

As they dance, it is quickly made clear that I was wrong. They stick to a basic step, a few spins, but mostly just looking into each other's eyes and holding each other. *Wow, Carl must really love him.*

They don't even make it through the full song before the DJ fades the music. Anthony is beet red, but laughing off his embarrassment. Carl is rubbing his back, laughing right along with him.

Dinner is served shortly after and I only just now realize that I have been trying to keep up with Eunice in terms of wine, which is a terrible idea on an empty stomach. Adam asks a server what the menu is for the night, and as I'm stuffing the bread she brought into my mouth to absorb whatever alcohol I had mindlessly sipped, I see Adam touch his phone to the back of his arm. He looks at some numbers on the screen, then pats his pocket. "I'll be right back." He stands, pausing for a moment to smile at me with my cheek puffed out like a chipmunk. "You look amazing tonight. Have I told you that yet?" He taps the back of my chair twice before heading off toward the restroom.

I turn away from watching him to see Carl and Anthony making their way to our table. Of course, they start with the most fun group when doing their rounds. We all stand to give hugs and well wishes. After a simple hug from Anthony, I get swept up in Carl's arms and pulled off the floor. "I am so glad you made it!" He sets me down and mimes brushing me off. "And that plus one of yours is..." He fans himself, eyeing over my shoulder to where Adam had disappeared off to. "So glad you dropped that Charlie guy. I knew you could do better."

My mouth opens and closes a few times. "I'm still with Charlie. He was just... busy tonight. Adam is my coworker."

Carl's face drops. "Oh, I am so sorry. I read that completely wrong." Anthony tugs at his arm. They have a lot of guests to get to. "I have to go, but know I support you in whatever decisions you make, even if I don't like the guy."

"Thanks..." is all I can get out before Carl is whisked away by his husband. I am still too stunned to sit back down, so I just watch them move on to the next table as I process it. It takes a lot for Carl not to like someone. He is hugging and sharing a laugh with Anthony's ex-boyfriend right now. Carl likes pretty much everyone, and pretty much everyone likes Carl. But Carl doesn't like Charlie, and Charlie doesn't like Carl...?

There is a gentle touch on my shoulder. "Coming or going?" Adam asks.

I flinch away, taking a second to register what was going on. That wine is hitting me all at once. "I... Staying. I'm just stretching my legs. How was the bathroom?"

He gives a confused laugh. "Uhh... fine? There's some really cool woodwork around the—are you okay?" He holds my arms, his hands warm on my skin.

I rub my face. "Yeah, fine. I'm just going to excuse myself for a moment." I push past him and make my way to the restroom. My reflection is ghost-white, not the usual blotchy red that comes with me drinking wine. Maybe I should cut myself off for the night.

I do my business, wash my hands, and splash water on my face. The room is not spinning, my vision is fine, and I still have feeling in my cheeks—I'm clearly not *drunk*. But why is my mind so hazy right now? And why did Carl's words trigger this reaction?

I stare myself down for a few moments before a knocking on the door brings me back to the present. I am at a wedding for one of my good friends. My plus one is out there alone with a bunch of strangers. There is going to be some amazing food waiting for me at that table. For some reason, the food is the motivation I need to get my butt in gear. I apologize to the two women waiting outside then head back to the dining area.

"Is everything good, honey?" Adam asks.

I freeze in sitting. *Honey?* I look straight ahead and there is Nate, sitting in his originally-assigned seat. Adam must have switched into boyfriend mode. It is such a relief that he is willing to go along with this. I let a smile cross my lips—not much acting involved, as him calling me 'honey' was actually quite endearing. "Everything's great.

I'm just in need of a bite to eat." I sit and look down at the salad that had been set at my place in my absence. "And this looks perfect."

CHAPTER 16

The Reception

While waiting for the main course and listening to the sweetest speeches by the couple's family and friends, Adam puts his hand around my shoulder. He leans in close and asks, "Is it alright if I do this?"

More than alright, I think, but I can only nod.

Dinner is amazing: the food, the drink, and the company (for the most part). Nate, however, is downing drinks faster than Eunice and is getting louder and bolder with each glass. We get through the meal with no issues, but shit hits the fan at dessert.

As the grooms are dancing with their mothers, we're given a small chocolate-covered shortbread cookie with a caramel drizzle—it looks like what would happen if you described a Twix bar to a five-star chef and asked him to make it—which makes sense since Carl's favorite candy is a Twix bar. The cake is still being used as decoration, it seems, so this will have to be my sweet until they finally get around to cutting it. It is *delicious.* The chocolate is a bit bitter, and I would have hated it on its own, but with the sweetness of the caramel and the buttery cookie? Heaven. Adam lightly taps his plate toward me.

"You sure?" I ask, my hands not hesitating in reaching out for it.

"Careful." Nate's voice is slurred. He is staring directly at Adam. "She's already a tease. Be a shame if she ended up *fat*, too." The f-word was slimy on his tongue—I'd told him about my body issues in college, and now he is using it as ammunition.

Adam sits up straighter. "Excuse me?" It is clear he had heard him but is daring Nate to repeat himself.

Nate laughs. "She's already gained, what, ten pounds since college?"

I load up a forkful of the fancy candy bar and let spite-fueled apathy spread across my face. "Twenty." I shove the food in my mouth. Somehow this bite tastes even better than the previous ones.

Adam's eyes don't leave Nate. His jaw is clenched. "You know what, Danielle? Once you finish that, I think it would be a great time to dance. A change of scenery seems to be in order."

I use my fork to scrape the remaining caramel off the plate, getting every last morsel as other guests make their way to the dance floor.

Adam stands and holds out his hand for me to take. I finish my glass of wine quickly—no way I'm leaving my beverage unaccompanied around Nate—and take his hand. Even though he only holds the ends of my fingers, I can feel his strength as he steadies me. He gives them a squeeze before letting go and holding out his hand again. "Cherry, would you care to join us?"

Cherry takes his hand, too. "Absolutely."

He leads us both to the dance floor, but Cherry veers off before we get there. She reappears balancing three shot glasses not twenty seconds later. "Liquid courage."

"Where did you get these?" I ask, taking one.

"Anthony's uncle is walking around with a tray of shot glasses and a bottle of tequila."

I shrug and shoot it. Not only was tequila my drink of choice in college, but this specific one goes down so smoothly, so I was able to keep a straight face with pretty minimal effort. I look over to see how Adam is reacting to it, hoping to get to poke fun at him this time. He is still holding his shot in his hand.

"Either of you ladies want this one? I'm going to have to pass."

The two drinks in rapid succession have me feeling bold. "What? Not strong enough for a tequila shot?"

"Actually, I don't want to risk a blood sugar spike. I already drank all the drinks I prepared for. Besides, I drove." He oscillates the shot between me and Cherry.

It finally hits me. "Oh my God, you're diabetic."

Adam gives a pressed-lip smile and nods, still offering the shot.

"Well, if you are saying it is medically necessary for me to take this shot for you..." I snatch the glass from his hand and shoot it. It goes down even easier than the first. "I am happy to carry that burden."

I plop the empty shot glasses on a nearby table and grab Adam and Cherry, dragging them to the center of the dance floor. I say the phrase "Holy shit I love this song!" at least five times in the first seven songs. Despite being a threesome, none of us ever feel left out of the dancing. Other people from our college group, including the grooms, join in with us at times, and we open the circle for them, having an overall blast. But as they come and go, we just keep to our spot on the dance floor.

The tempo changes and the DJ switches to a slow song. Without a word, Cherry backs away, leaving Adam and me alone. He holds out his hand for me to take. Just two friends having an amazing time at a wedding, why shouldn't we slow dance? I take his hand and he places his other hand on my waist.

"Is this alright?" he asks.

"Yeah," I whisper, pulling myself closer and placing my free hand on his shoulder. He shifts his hand to the small of my back, keeping our other hands joined. Once we work out how to situate ourselves, I bring my eyes up to meet his and something just... clicks. Being so close to him feels good. His hand on my back feels good. My hand in his feels good. Looking up into his eyes feels good. *Adam* feels good. We stand there for a moment, not even moving as the song becomes recognizable as one by Ed Sheeran.

Adam starts to move side to side and I sway with him. I look at our joined hands to see how perfectly mine fits into his. It's strange how new this feeling is, this sense that there is no better place for me to be right now, that out of every possible outcome for this night, I ended up with the perfect one. I am about to rest my head on Adam's chest when I have a wave of clarity. *Charlie.* The one thought makes me pull away, letting out a nervous laugh. "Actually, I think this might be a good time to take a breather."

As if on cue, a waiter walks by with a tray of the specialty cocktails for the night—he tells me it's Anthony's parents' pick, a Sazerac, but I'm already a sip in by the time he finishes his spiel. I thank him before wandering back over to Adam, who is making his way off the dance floor. I leave a gap between us as we walk back to the table together.

After a few more sips and quietly watching the party rage around us, I finally speak up. "I'm sorry about that."

Adam shares a warm smile. "No apologies needed. I can't say that I wasn't disappointed, but I understand."

My head is swimming as it tries to process what he said. *He wasn't disappointed? No. Wait. He CAN'T say he wasn't disappointed. So that means he WAS disappointed.* I stare at him while he people-watches. *Was he feeling the same thing?*

Adam turns to face me, his eyes going wide to see me already looking directly at him. "Do you mind if I ask what's the deal with the creepy guy?"

Normally I would dance around this question, but *for some reason,* my inhibitions are bypassed at the moment, so I just lay it on him. "Nate doesn't know the meaning of 'no.'" I take a long sip of my drink, not that I really need it at this point. "At one point after a movie night and some drinking with a bunch of friends, he refused to leave my apartment. It was just me and him and Cherry left. I was asking him to leave for about an hour, but he kept on insisting on staying and that Cherry should leave. I even tried to leave the apartment myself, but he stood in the doorway, so I 'went to the bathroom' and called the cops."

Adam shakes his head in shock. "But he was still invited to the wedding?"

I shrug it off, taking another sip to drown the icky feeling I get whenever I remember that night. "I didn't really tell anyone about that incident. Besides, I think Nate and Anthony are cousins, so he might have just gotten the relative invite."

"Well, I hope my presence here as your fake boyfriend is making you feel a bit more at ease."

"Your presence here makes me feel *so* at ease." *Maybe too at ease.*

CHAPTER 17

The DD

I am having so much fun with Adam that I can't help but imagine if this were real life. After a few too many daydreams, I realize it is not helping me stay in the moment of having fun at my friend's wedding. I decide on a plan: every time I think of Adam as more than a friend, I take a drink. It is a great distraction. I lose track of drinks fairly quickly, but the buzz is just what I need to enjoy the rest of the night with my friends without worrying about how dashingly handsome Adam looks in that suit. *Especially his butt. Wow, those pants look great on him.* I take another drink. *But they might look better on my hotel room floor.* Another. *Does this even have alcohol in it? I can't taste it.* See? No longer thinking about Adam. Perfect distraction.

I get to the shuttle in a giant mess of drunks wearing party clothes on a night growing ever colder, but nobody looks chilly. I am warmed by the concoctions mingling in my belly.

Adam is waiting off to the side. He walked me part-way, then said goodnight. It seems like he both wants to make sure I make it on the bus alright, while also giving me my space. It might be for the best, because everything in me wants to give him a kiss goodnight. That's what you do at the end of an amazing date, right?

I'm glancing over at him one more time when I notice a look of concern on his face. He's not looking at me, but behind me in line. I look back to see Nate in line for the same shuttle. *Shit.* When I turn my gaze back to Adam, he is already halfway to me.

"I would feel more comfortable if you allowed me to drive you back to your hotel." He is holding my hand in his.

"I would feel like that, too."

I use him for support as we walk back to the parking area. Despite his car not being a piece of crap like mine, it is the crummiest car in the lot. Like, surrounded by cars I only ever saw on those car shows my dad likes. The gravel catches me off-guard more than once, my heels slipping to the point I cling to Adam so I don't fall. I tell myself it wouldn't be any easier if I hadn't been drinking.

Adam opens the passenger door for me, and I barely miss hitting my head on the frame. *I'm not drunk, though. I'm basically sober.* A burp comes up, a little too acidic for my comfort. *But I'm still totally good.*

We drive out and down the wooded, winding road. The car is silent, probably because Adam is concentrating so hard on the unlit serpent of asphalt.

One lapse of consciousness later, freeway lights are whizzing past me in a steady rhythm.

"Good morning, sleeping beauty." Adam laughs, keeping his eyes on the road. "How much did you drink tonight?"

I roll my eyes, but the car spinning around me doesn't help with the nausea. "I swear... not drunk."

"You can't even say a complete sentence." He hands me his phone open to Spotify.

I stealthily take a deep breath. "I swear to drunk, Adam, I'm not God."

His eyes narrow. "I can't tell if that was a joke or not."

"That's for me to know and you to find out." The bite of flirtation in my tone is not intentional, but I enjoy the sound. I like Adam, and I think he likes me, too. I turn on some top hits playlist, too tired to search around. *Tired. Yeah, that's what I am.*

The rest of the drive is a blur. I fully come to as we pull into the drop off area of my hotel. That last power nap seems to have come with amazing clarity. I know what I want. I want Adam.

I take hold of the door handle but pause. "Do you think you can walk me up to my room?"

Without hesitation, Adam is out his door and asking the valet if he can leave his car here for a second. My heart is racing—totally excitement and not at all dehydration. But why am I so excited? *Oh my God, he's coming up to my hotel room.* A dumb smile is painted on my face as Adam helps me out of the car.

We go up the elevator in silence, but he hasn't let go of my hand. Every few seconds, his thumb rubs over my knuckles. We get to the door and I fiddle in my bag for my room key. I find it quickly, but don't take it out right away. "Thanks for making sure I got back safely."

"Of course. Anything for my..." He looks deep into my eyes. "Anything for you."

I lean in close, going onto my tiptoes. Adam leans down. My heart flutters in my chest. I can feel his breath on my lips, it smells like peppermint. I close my eyes and lean the last bit, but stumble forward. I open my eyes to see that Adam had stepped away.

"This isn't a good idea, Danielle." He lets go of my hand. "I'm sorry."

I watch as he walks back to the elevators and disappears around the corner, my jaw slack the whole time. *What just happened?*

Bile rises in my throat and I book it into my room. Adam's actions are making me physically sick. That is clearly the only explanation.

After a quick visit to the porcelain goddess, I crash on the bed. It is cozy, I am exhausted, but my brain keeps replaying that last moment with Adam.

Was it something I said? Something I did? Did I misread everything? No. No, the signs were there and clear—the man had just eaten a mint. He's the jerk. He's the tease. Oh, no. Am I Nate in this situation? No. He clearly leaned in, too, right?

I pull out my phone to charge it and see two messages: one from Adam and one from Charlie. I open Charlie's first. I'm mad at Adam.

> Charlie: you do you. we can talk when we're both home.

Yes. Charlie. Charlie is my constant. I know he likes me. We've been together for years. He is a sure thing.

> Danielle: Back at the hotel. Be home tomorrow.

I switch over to Adam's message.

Adam: I'd really like to talk through what happened tonight. Whether it's tomorrow on the drive to Portland or another time, I'll leave that up to you.

I switch to my browser and check train times. Before I know it, I've purchased a 9:50 am ticket back to Portland.

Danielle: There's nothing to talk about. I don't need a ride anymore. I'll see you back at work.

I glance at the time. 2:04 am.

Danielle: Happy Easter.

CHAPTER 18

The Fight

My alarm is blaring and my heartbeat is pounding in my head. Maybe I *was* a bit intoxicated yesterday. I try to scan through the night in my mind. At first, I can only recall a feeling: Adam bad, Charlie good. But why?

I remember Adam holding my hand in the elevator. *Oh, God...* I turn over in bed to see the other pillow untouched, not sure if I'm relieved or disappointed.

I look through my phone for more clues. I see a loving message to Charlie and an abrupt one to Adam. *Why didn't I need a ride anymore?* It takes me a few seconds to recall buying the train ticket. I confirm the memory with the confirmation message in my email. The ticket is for 9:50 am and it is currently... *Shit!* I throw my stuff into my bag and request a rideshare as I unload my last stomachful in the toilet.

I make it to the train just in time. As I watch the world zoom by, the previous night reveals itself to me in bits and pieces. By the time we hit the Columbia River, I have the puzzle pretty much figured out.

I had essentially fallen in love with Adam last night and been shot down. Hard. I was angry, but now I'm embarrassed. I misread his kindness as interest. He was being a good friend, and I repaid him by trying to kiss him. If I had just taken the shuttle home, that would have been the best night of the year. Instead, I screwed it up.

My phone vibrates with a message. I hope it's Adam. *No, I hope it's Charlie.* Instead, it's my landlord, Susan.

> Susan: Just a 24-hour warning—I'll be showing your place on Monday at 3:00pm. Putting a written notice in your box, but it didn't look like you were home, so I thought I'd give you a heads-up.

I sit up straight. I'd been so busy settling into first-year teaching that I told Charlie to take care of rent stuff. Did he not renew the lease? I don't remember ever signing anything... I dial Susan, my foot tapping with anxiety until she picks up.

"Hello, Danielle. Does Monday not work for you? They said they were free all week, so I can reschedule." I love the sound of her voice, like the host of a preschool show without being condescending.

"No, Susan, I'm so sorry, but Charlie and I just forgot to renew, it seems." I'm trying to sound calm, but with a rough night of sleep last night, my brain is telling me that now is the time to cry.

"I just spoke with Charles last week. He told me you two found a new place and were giving up the unit. I know July is a ways away, but the rental market is hot right now."

Found a new place? Was he trying to surprise me with a new apartment and I just ruined it? A light comes on. *Is it the building we used to go by when we would walk to get coffee last summer? The one I told him I'd love to live in?* "Oh, I'm so sorry, Susan. It must have slipped my mind. Yes. Tomorrow is fine. I'll be sure it's tidy and make myself scarce for the afternoon."

"Thank you, love. I'll be sad to see you two go, but I hope you make a great life for yourselves in Indiana."

Indiana? I sit there with the phone to my ear long after Susan hangs up. I rideshare home in a haze much different from my drunken buzz the night before.

I drop my bag on the floor once I walk into my place and sit, considering everything. I was willing to throw away everything with Charlie when a glimmer of something better came my way. Even if that glimmer was false, even if Adam only saw me as a friend, being treated with respect was so novel to me for some reason.

The front door opens at 10 pm. I barely let him take one step in before I speak. "You chose not to renew our lease without even talking to me?"

"And you went to a wedding with some other guy!" He doesn't even have to shift his facial expression—he came in mad.

"I went to the wedding with a co-worker after you refused to go."

"A co-worker who probably has a crush on you. I know you two spend time together every week."

"With our classes! He doesn't even like me like that!"

"He's attracted to women. Of course he's attracted to you."

I'm taken aback when I realize this is the first compliment he's given me in probably months. "Amanda is attracted to women. You were fine with me going with her."

A creepy smile finds its way to his face and, for the moment, he looks a lot like Nate. "That's different. If you two hooked up, it would be hot."

I stare in shock. "Are you kidding me right now?"

His silent stare says it all.

I grab my bag off the floor and push past Charlie, taking the keys from his hand. "I'll be at my dad's."

"You don't even want to see the place I picked out for us?" he asks as I step out the door.

"Not if it's in Indi-fucking-ana!" I slam the door behind me. *Where did that come from? I've never swore in a fight with Charlie before. I've never even yelled at him before.*

I start on my way to my dad's house, but the gas light comes on immediately. Closest gas station? A block from Amanda and Bea's place. I shoot a text before I get out to fill up.

> Danielle: Hope you and Bea are both doing alright. Sorry for not checking in yet. Busy weekend. Let me know if you two need anything.

By the time I'm back in my car, I already have a response.

> Amanda: Good busy or bad busy?
> Danielle: Long story busy.

I can't even shift into drive before she gets back to me.

> Amanda: I'm going to need the story ASAP.
> Amanda: I love Bea, but she is boring AF when con-

cussed.

Danielle: Be there in 5.

It's more like two minutes, but I linger in my car for a bit to be more on time.

Danielle: Here. Don't want to knock in case the patient is sleeping.

Not a minute later, Amanda is sneaking out of her front door. She hops in the passenger seat.

"Bea is resting in a dark room with an audiobook on as quiet as possible and her phone is dialed to me so I'm one press away. Tell. Me. Everything."

Where do I even start? "Charlie is a complete and total ass."

Amanda's face is flat. "So you finally took off those rose-colored glasses, huh?"

"He decided, on his own, that we are moving out of state, and told the landlord not to renew our lease."

"No shit?"

"Yeah, I found out a few hours ago when my landlord asked if she could show the place tomorrow."

"Wow, I thought the story was going to be about the wedding."

I let out a groan. "That's its own can of worms. I think I ruined my friendship with Adam."

She seems even more intrigued by this information. "Oh, no. I got your text about him taking you to Seattle. Did something happen on the drive?"

"No. He actually came to the wedding with me when I found out someone I didn't want to be around was there. He saved my skin."

Amanda is quiet for a beat. "Was he weird about it being a gay wedding?"

"No, no. He was cool with it. We had a ton of fun."

She holds out her hands, palms up. "You're going to have to paint me a clearer picture here... How does any of this lead to ruining a friendship?"

I rub my hands down my face and groan. "I tried to kiss him."

She turns her whole body to me. "Holy shit, I knew—wait. Tried?"

I give a pressed-lip smile. "He rejected me."

Amanda's eyes get wide. "Woah, woah, woah. That was not how I read his feelings toward you at all. Did he explain why?"

I shrug. "He just said it was a bad idea and left."

"What? Why was it a bad idea? Because you work together? Because—"

"Because he doesn't like me, obviously," I finish for her, starting to cry. "Because the only people interested in me are assholes and creeps."

Amanda wraps her arms around me as best she can with the center console in the way. "I'm sure that's not the case."

I'm wailing now, snot pouring from my nose. "It is! And I have to stay with the asshole or be alone my whole life!" I stop crying as I come to a realization. *Is that why I've stayed with him? So I wouldn't be alone?*

Amanda vocalizes my next thought. "Might it be better to just be alone?"

After spending the rest of the break at my dad's house, I'm ready to face Charlie. I've ignored his calls and texts, wanting some distance to think things through, but at this point I sort of have to see him in order to have access to my work clothes and computer.

He's sitting at his desk, gaming headset on, yelling at his teammates. I'd try to sneak past him, but he gets extra startled when he's amped up like this. I close the door hard and he turns to face me. He looks exhausted. Maybe he's had a hard time sleeping without me here? He holds up a finger, telling me to wait, so I do. It takes him five more minutes to finish the round, but then he takes a deep breath and faces me.

"You know I can't stay in Portland. I hate it here. Plus Indiana is so much cheaper."

"Then you are welcome to go to Indiana. I'm staying here. My dad says I can stay with him until I figure something out."

"You're really just going to give up on us like that? Choose a place over your boyfriend?"

"I'm choosing my life over you. And you're choosing this move over me." I have no fight in me, and it seems neither does he. "You can stay here until the lease is up. I'll move out over the next few weeks."

"Fine." He turns back to his game, headset on.

Part of me worries about how he'll do on his own—where he'll get money or a way over there—but most of me knows it's not my problem anymore. He is an adult making adult decisions and I am an adult ready to begin my adult life.

CHAPTER 19

The Return

My forehead is planted on my desk, hair fanning out around me. It's Friday morning, half an hour before the students arrive. I've managed to avoid Adam so far this week—even at the staff meeting, which took some careful maneuvering of slipping in late and running to the restroom right as it ended. But today is both Mass and Reading Buddies. My students are so giddy to see their buddies again. I'm... I wouldn't say *giddy*... more nervous, actually. I don't want that awkward conversation, but I do want my friend back.

There's a knock on my open door and I shoot up. My eyes take a second to adjust, revealing Adam in my doorway.

"Can we talk?" he asks.

No. "Yeah, sure." I stand, straightening out my mess of hair and skirt. "Can I go first, though?"

He mimes zipping his lips.

My heart is racing. *I love you.* "I'm sorry. I got too drunk and did something I wouldn't have if I had my head on straight. I am so happy to have you as a friend and I would hate it if my actions ruined that."

Adam takes a step back, giving a weak smile. "Friends, then."

I feel the weight lift off my shoulders, even though it's not the complete truth. I am happy to have him as a friend, but I would be even happier if he were more—if only he wanted that, too. "I'd love it if we could just forget everything that happened at the hotel."

"Consider it forgotten." He pulls me in for a hug and it lingers just a moment or two longer than a typical friendly hug, long enough for me to get a good sniff of his clothes. The scent relaxes me, and with it, I am ready for the day.

"We'll do a quick bathroom trip, then meet you in the main hall-way?"

"And then buddies at 2:15?"

"I'd say we're buddies all the time, but we can meet up at 2:15, sure."

He gives a half-laugh at the joke, then leaves, passing Amanda in the doorway. She shimmies in.

"So, you two are still friends?" she asks.

"It looks like it." I move to the whiteboard to write out the plan for the day.

"Did you tell him that you and Charlie broke up?"

"It didn't come up."

"Oh. Shame." She walks back toward the door, but pauses. "Are you going to Easter drinks after work today?" We didn't have a staff get-together before break because it was a solemn day, so Mark decided a post-Easter happy hour was in order.

"Yeah, why?"

"I need to talk to you about something."

I finish writing "Reading Buddies" on the schedule and turn to see her with a huge smile on her face and her left hand held in front of her. The spring sun glints off of something, catching my eye.

"No way!" I want to ask more, but the bell rings, and Amanda hurries away before I can get another word out.

She avoids my attempts at eye contact during Mass, but I can see a cheeky grin on her face. She is really going to leave me hanging, huh?

I manage to sneak a few outgoing texts, trying to get more information, but I can't hunt her down in person because I'm covering recess duties for Cheryl's long-term sub while she finds her footing.

Cheryl's healthy, bouncing baby girl came on Easter morning. They named her May, which was an unexpected choice for a child born in April, but to each their own. It sent a pang of sadness through me when I'd heard, but then a glow of hope followed: I am no longer with the person who does not want children. I may not be with someone who does right now, but I am free to find him.

But now I'm outside watching the middle schoolers push some boundaries, second guessing if I'd want to deal with adolescence. I pull Brady over to have a talk about his roughhousing. I try to keep it lighter, as he responds better when he doesn't feel like he's about to be punished, so I end it on a positive note.

"You excited for Reading Buddies today?"

He looks over to his friends, seemingly desperate to rejoin them, but answers my question anyway. "Yeah, sure. I guess."

I wave him away. "We can be done if you want. Go back to your posse. Just remember to keep your hands to yourself."

He starts to jog off but then turns back around. "Miss Monroe, can I ask you something?"

"Sure, what's up?" I scan over the blacktop, making sure he's not just trying to distract me from something.

"Do you like Mr. Johnson?" It isn't teasing or poking fun, his tone is genuinely curious.

My face starts to blush, but I feign innocence. "Of course. Don't *you* like Mr. Johnson?"

Brady's expression falls flat. "Miss Monroe, his last name is Johnson and the class has yet to make a single joke about it. I think that tells you how much we like him."

One hand rises to cover the cackle of a laugh that slips out and my other shoos Brady away. Middle schoolers. Maybe they do have a bright side.

When the seventh graders come in for buddies, the first graders are ecstatic. They all have books picked out that they want to read, and most have decided *they* want to do the reading—even some of my lowest readers have early reader texts that they've been practicing all week just to show off to their buddies.

Adam walks in last, two large, identical books in his hand. The seventh graders stare at me with knowing smiles, and Adam has the same conniving look on his face.

"Nope!" I say, backing away. The seventh graders laugh.

He holds up the book so I can see the cover. I was right. It's *Twilight*. "Yes. It's time." He turns to his class. "I told you she would love the idea."

I let out a sigh in a laugh. "I'm sorry, I'm already reading something." Leaning back onto my desk, I pull out the first book I find. *Biscuit Goes to School*. A student accidentally tore a page and put it there so I can tape it. "Going to take me the entire half hour to finish reading it..." I wave the picture book in front of his face. It can't be more than a dozen pages, and each page has about one sentence.

He pulls the book from my hand. "You chose the last three books. It's my turn."

I groan, but hold out my hands.

"You knew it was coming. We can't talk this much smack about a book without ever reading it." He gives me the nicer copy. He always does.

"Fine. I'll start it now so it can be over faster." We sit and I open my copy. There's writing on the inside of the cover. "To my Bella, from your Edward." I look up at Adam in horror. What happened to us forgetting about the hotel? And *why* would he choose those two to emulate?

Adam notices my face and scrunches his brow.

"You want to explain this to me?" I ask, turning the page around.

I've come to find that Adam has two laughs. One light, charming laugh that comes mostly as a smile, and another booming cackle that I'd only ever heard a handful of times, most of which were at the wedding. What comes out of his mouth now is the latter. It takes him half a minute to catch his breath before he can finally gasp out a response. "I got it at the used bookstore." Then he goes off again.

At this point, the seventh graders are staring at him, probably wondering if I broke him somehow. It really isn't *that* funny, but his reaction is hilarious to me, so I struggle to keep a straight face.

My solution is to walk to the window and get some fresh air and give Adam a chance to cool off, too. He is able to pull himself together pretty quickly once I'm gone, and when I turn back around, his nose is already in the book. Some seventh graders are still eyeing me skeptically, but they slowly go back to listening to their buddies read.

I walk around the room a few times, listening to some of my students read with so much pride. It warms my heart. When I go back to my desk, the book is waiting for me. I look at the message scrawled in permanent marker, noticing the handwriting is not too horrible. I then realize that these two were not actually destined for eternity—there is no way it would be at a used book store if they were still together. *I mean, if Adam and I ended up together, I don't think I would get rid of...* My mind takes that as a cue to have a drink, but alas, we are in an elementary school classroom. But it does remind me... "Are you going to Easter drinks?"

He keeps his eyes on his page. "Have I ever *not* gone to a staff happy hour?"

"Nope. Want to share fries?"

He turns a page. "I was actually thinking fish and chips. My body is now expecting to have fish on Fridays. But you're welcome to poach some fries."

"Is it still poaching if I have permission?"

The question finally takes him away from the book. "Fine, then you are *not* welcome to poach some fries..." He raises his eyebrows suggestively.

I chuckle and finally start to read, even though we have only a few minutes left before both of our classes need to pack up.

The moment our classes are dismissed, I turn to Amanda and whisper through gritted teeth. "Tell me *everything.*"

She takes my hand and pulls me inside, giggling like a schoolgirl. Once we're in my room with the door closed, she lets out a squeal. "I wanted to leave you in suspense until we were at the bar, but I'm too excited! I don't even know where to start, so ask me a question."

"I... uh..." I snap my fingers, trying to find words. Amanda looks like she's about to burst and I need to help her get words out so she doesn't. "When did this happen?"

"Last night! I was packing my bag for today and I turn around and *BAM!* She's on one knee!"

I run up to hug her, and she's basically vibrating in my arms. "Congratulations!"

"Thanks!" She backs away, fiddling with her ring. "But you should ask... more questions." Her voice now has a more serious tone.

I'm trying to figure out more questions, but all the ones that come to me are reasons to be excited—setting a date, telling her parents... Then it hits me. "Are you leaving the school?"

Amanda bites her lip and nods. "I was offered a job at a public school for next year. That's why Bea finally proposed—she knew my job was the only thing standing in the way of me saying yes."

I hug her again, a little more subdued this time. "I'm still so happy for you. But I'm sure lots of people in the school community would have helped you fight the archdiocese if they tried to fire you."

"I know, but I don't think I have a lot of fight in me right now. I just want to be somewhere that I can be with Bea and not worry about losing my job. Lord knows we have enough to worry about right now." She starts to cry in my arms.

I squeeze her tighter. "Feel what you need to feel right now, but once you're ready, there are free drinks waiting for us and I need you to tell me *every* idea you have for your wedding."

We stand there for another minute or two as Amanda rides out her emotions, then grab our stuff and head over to O'Connor's.

Everyone else is already there. Adam has a huge plate of fish and chips in front of him and the first thing I do is steal a fry. He pretends to guard his plate as I approach, but it isn't hard to sneak around him. Amanda and I go off on our own at first, and she shows me her wedding Pinterest board.

"The first pins are from ages ago, before I even realized I was a lesbian, then you'll notice a huge uptick about a week after Bea and I started dating..."

We scroll through and about every three pins I point and go, "Ooh, I like that." She really has great taste.

Soon, Principal Miller comes up behind us and pats Amanda on the back. "Did you want to tell everyone what you told me today, as long as we're all here?"

Amanda nods. "I'll tell them the first part, not sure if I'm ready for the second part."

"Totally up to you." He turns, using a fork he grabbed off our table to clink against his pint. "Hey everyone, real quick, before people start to leave, Amanda has an announcement."

She stands up and addresses the room. "I am really sad to have to say this, but I am choosing not to renew for next year, and am moving to one of the public schools. I love you all so much and will miss every single one of you." She turns back to the table, then changes her mind and turns back around. "Oh! And I'm getting married! To my girlfriend. Who I love very much." She holds out her hand to show off her engagement ring.

There are looks of shock all around the room. As the shock dissipates, most people seem to be genuinely happy for Amanda. There are a few sour faces, but they are smart enough to not ruin the moment.

It is clear that Alice already knew about Amanda and Bea, or at least suspected it, and she is the first to wrap her in a huge congratulatory hug.

The three of us drink together as everyone else trickles out. Adam sneaks over to give a congratulations as he leaves for the night.

Alice turns to me. "What was that?"

"What was what?" I turn around, thinking something must have flown by or fallen or something.

"Mr. Johnson just gave you quite the look."

"A look? What look?"

Amanda pipes in. "Thank you! He looks at her like she's the most special thing in the world." She holds out her hand. "Not that you're not! I love you. But it's a very *want-y* kind of look."

I shake my head. "No. He doesn't like me like that."

Alice shares a look with Amanda. "Mmhmm. Right."

"I'm really just here trying not to ruin our friendship, so, if you two could stop with—" I gesture wildly between them, "—whatever this is, that would be great."

They both slowly sip their drinks, making faces at each other.

I end up sleeping on Amanda and Bea's couch. We drank quite a bit and I am not paying for a rideshare all the way out to my dad's and I sure as hell am not going back to Charlie's place, even if half of my stuff is still there. After a few board games, the happy engaged couple heads off to bed, but I am having trouble sleeping. I turn on a lamp and pull out the only book I have on me, just to help lull me to sleep.

It doesn't work. It's like being a teenager again, reliving the absolutely insane emotions that come with first love. There's also a kick of serious nostalgia from watching the movies when I was in middle school. It's so bad. I hate it. But at the same time, *I love it*. I'm halfway through the entire book before I look at my watch and see that it's three in the morning and I force myself to finally get to sleep.

CHAPTER 20

The Saga

It's Reading Buddies time again. Every single one of my students wants to try reading to their buddies this week. I am so proud of them and how their confidence has skyrocketed. The benefits of having a safe big kid to support them are astonishing.

Adam walks in with *Twilight* in his hands and a reusable shopping tote slung over his shoulder.

"That was the *worst* book I have ever read." He tosses his copy onto my desk. "But I also loved it and I cannot *wait* for you to finish it so we can discuss."

I hold up my copy. "I finished it on Tuesday, and also love-hated it."

He pulls up a tiny first-grader chair and sits on it. The tallest person in the room in the shortest chair—it's a fantastic picture. "I read the whole thing over the weekend. Is it weird admitting that?"

I shake my head. "Not at all. They put crack between the pages or something, I swear."

"More like heroin." He pauses to see if I catch the joke.

"Our own personal brand?" I say with a side-eye.

"Hey, you got it!" He reaches into his bag and pulls out two more identical books—*New Moon*. "So, naturally, we are going to finish the series before the end of the school year, right?"

I snag a copy. "Entirely for research purposes, of course."

He shrugs. "Of course. We have to see if Twilight is a one-off or if all of them are laced with drugs."

I laugh, setting the book on my desk to do a lap of the classroom. Stepping over the legs of kids sitting on the floor, I realize it was so much easier to navigate this maze at the beginning of the school year. Some of those seventh graders have hit major growth spurts, while the first graders all grew at least an inch. None of them quite have the spatial awareness to keep their limbs contained.

When I come back, Adam is already a page or two into the book.

My eyes are in pain from rolling so hard. *It's not that hard to get over a guy, Bella. You're better off without someone who thinks he knows what's best for you.* But, of course, I can't stop reading. It's like gossip—I know it's bad for me, but I really *really* want to know what happens.

It takes me a little longer to read the second book, as end-of-year assessments are taking their toll. I stay up late on Thursday night to squeeze in the last few pages and go to sleep pleasantly satiated.

Friday afternoon, Adam has a copy of the next book. We both commit to taking two weeks for this one, as it is a little more dense and we didn't realize how taxing this time of year is on teachers.

Everyone told me it's all downhill from Spring Break, and partially they are right—time seems to be speeding by. But at the same time, there is a lot of stuff we still have to finish. My class is about two weeks behind in Math, so I'm trying to figure out how we'll be squeezing a four-week geometry unit into two weeks, but still have it properly assessed before grades are due. Amanda is a Godsend and stayed after school with me to let me know what they do and do not need covered before they move on to second grade. But even with her help, I still feel like I'm in over my head; like I'm back at the beginning of the school year having no idea what I'm doing.

Thankfully, every night, I get to escape into a world that doesn't have grading, schedules, classroom management, or that pesky spring cold that every student insists on telling me that they have while standing two inches away from my face. I now understand the kids who locked themselves in their rooms to read and avoid the real world.

We agree to three weeks for the final book—and that takes us to the final Reading Buddies of the year. We still have school next week, but the final Friday is barely even a half day, so we won't have time to meet.

I didn't think I could love my students any more than I already did, but whenever I imagine them leaving for second grade next year, I start to tear up. I mean, they'll be right down the hall, but they won't be *my* kiddos anymore. They'll belong to whoever takes over for Amanda. Thinking about Amanda leaving makes me well up even more.

I'm in the middle of one of these emotional swells when Amanda comes in Friday morning. "Hey, did I interrupt something?"

I wipe my eyes. No tears have fallen quite yet, but they are threatening to. "No. Just thinking about you leaving."

She bites her lip. "Well, I do have some news on that front. The school I'm moving to has another opening posted. First grade!"

I shift over in my seat and open my laptop, then I pause. I haven't applied to any other jobs so far this spring. I told myself it was because I was just too busy and would do it over the summer, but part of me just... didn't want to. "Actually, as much as I'd love to be school besties again, I think I'm going to stick it out here for a bit. Find my footing as a teacher before having to learn a new school and curriculum." I scrunch up my face. "I'm sorry."

Amanda shakes it off. "No apologies. I totally get it. It's going to be like I'm a first-year teacher all over again. Definitely not something I'm looking forward to." She starts to move toward the door but stops in her tracks. "Actually, another thing. Bea and I were hoping to save up some money for the wedding and were considering renting out the second bedroom since we no longer need it to claim we're 'just roommates.' We'd love to rent to someone we know, and I'm pretty sure you're sick of commuting from your dad's."

"If it means I still get to see you every day, I'm so in." I sigh. "Also, I love my dad, but moving back home after being on my own for years is *rough*."

"We'll need a bit of time to clear out the space, but how about we say July for move-in?"

"Perfect."

And just like that, my day is starting off on a fantastic note. Now, I get to ride this little high until we get to Reading Buddies and I get to spend time with my other best friend, talking about the ending to this series we've been reading for almost two months now while our students eat treats and hang out with their buddies to celebrate the end of the year.

Adam arrives with his class, a two-liter of soda, and some plastic cups.

I elbow him. "You get to clean up if anyone spills."

He sets down the drinks and waves me off. "Oh, your first graders are super responsible."

"I wasn't talking about them." I gesture my head to the seventh graders who are tripping over themselves just to make it through the classroom.

Adam gets serious for a second. "I will make them clean up any spills." His eyes narrow as he considers his class. "And then I'll do a secondary clean to make sure they get it all."

"Thank you." I open all the goodies and let the students pick out what they want. The first graders are so excited to show their buddies the cards they made for them this week. My heart aches as I realize that these buddies won't be together again. Next year, my kids buddy up with sixth grade, while the soon-to-be eighth graders will get Kindergarteners. The year after that, the big kids are off to high school. I'm glad they get this time to just hang out together, though, and end this chapter on the right note.

Adam and I sit at the treats table, *Breaking Dawn* out in front of us.

"Team Edward or Team Jacob?" Adam asks. We made sure to avoid this question until the very end, as neither of us had enough information to make a committed decision.

"Am I allowed to say 'neither?'" I ask.

"You have to say a character name. For example, I am Team Charlie. Just a single dad trying to raise his daughter in the most confusing time in her life, and supporting her as best he can throughout. He was her healthiest relationship."

I nod. "I do love Charlie, but I think I would be Team Bella. She really needed to choose herself and not let everything be dictated by this decision between two guys. Like, step away for a bit. It's not like Edward or Jacob were going anywhere." I roll my eyes, hopefully for the last time as we close this saga. "But now, which is better: the books or the movies?"

Adam doesn't hesitate in his response. "The books. Hands-down."

"And the reason?"

"I was forced to watch the movies by an ex who took it *way* too seriously." He strokes the book in front of him with his thumb, then looks up at me. "I was given a chance to read the books by a friend who laughed through it with me. Much more enjoyable."

"Well, I *was* going to say I liked the movies more because it was less time out of my life, but I think I like your answer so much that I'm going to switch to books."

"Fair. But now, do we move on to *Midnight—*"

I put my hand on his book to stop him from saying anything else. "Nope! I'm good with moving onto another series."

We discuss books we might want to tackle over the summer, but decide to think on it until end-of-year drinks next week. Grades are due Monday night, so our weekends are going to be booked solid with grading and comment-writing, but I know that I'm going to spend whatever free time I have searching for another series to suggest.

CHAPTER 21

The End of the Year

I t's time for end-of-year drinks at O'Connor's and I am leading the charge. My students spent their final few hours of school cleaning the classroom. All of our materials are stored away in closets, butcher paper is covering the bookshelves so they don't accumulate dust, and the desks and chairs are neatly stacked along one wall so the floors can be waxed. All I have to do now is begin the process of de-stressing, and that begins with some drinks.

The weather is fantastic—it's our first day above 80 degrees this year, so I shed the cardigan and head out in my lightweight blouse and skirt. Amanda told me to go on ahead since she has to do a little extra housekeeping before she hands in her keys, so Adam is walking over with me to grab some tables.

"Wait, like an entire handle of whiskey?" Adam asks.

"Yeah, he could barely carry the gift bag through the door! Apparently, his uncle owns a distillery or something so they thought it would be a good end-of-year gift." I laugh, remembering how close Ricky had been to dropping the bag on the floor. That would have been a fun smell to try to get out of the rug.

"I guess it makes sense—they give you wine when you have two weeks off, and hard liquor when you have two months off."

"Oh, no, I still got some bottles of wine, too. It's going to be a great summer."

It's barely afternoon, so the pub is practically empty. We didn't need to swing over so early, but we make the most of it by having a drink in our hands by the time the others arrive. We settle on a few books to read over the summer, then join in conversations with our other coworkers, commiserating over the rough patches we went through this year. We all agree that fifth grade had it worst, especially when they went through a strange phase of licking the handrails whenever they used the stairs. They also had the highest number of students taking sick days. Weird how that works.

Amanda finally arrives and joins us at a table. Time flies by. Pretty soon, the parents among us leave to go take care of their children, Mark closes the group tab, and the rest start to depart. Nobody leaves without a heartfelt goodbye to Amanda, even the ones who were not so pleased with her engagement announcement—it's hard not to love her.

In the end, it's just Adam, Amanda, and me, and I couldn't be happier. My two favorite people in the whole building. I'm also pleasantly three beers in—a little buzz, but I still have my wits about me. I switch to water regardless; I don't think my body would appreciate a repeat of what happened the night of the wedding.

After a quick trip to the restroom, I return to see Adam and Amanda talking quietly. I try to make out what they're saying, but the after-work crowd has shown up and I can't hear anything through the din. Adam looks at me, then back at Amanda, confused.

As I sit down, Amanda stands up. "My turn for the restroom!" Her tone is weirdly cheerful for someone who is just going to go pee...

Adam watches her go, then turns to me. "How's Charlie?" he asks.

Now it's my turn to look confused. "Uh, he's *your* favorite character. But I guess he's... happy? He has a great relationship with his dau—"

Adam cuts in. "No, not him. Your boyfriend. Amanda told me to ask you how your boyfriend Charlie is doing."

What is that woman up to? "Uh... we broke up over Spring Break."

Adam sits with the information for a few beats. "Not because of me, right?"

"No. He saw the relationship going a certain way and I was no longer on board. I chose myself over the relationship."

"Team Danielle?" he asks.

"Yeah, Team Danielle."

"Good. I'm happy for you." He holds up his glass. "To Team Danielle."

I hold up my water, but a hand shoots out and snatches it from me. Amanda's eyes are wide as she holds my glass. "*Never* toast with water!" She hands me her drink instead.

I raise it and go back to the toast. "To Team Danielle."

Amanda jumps on my back and hugs me from behind, yelling "Team Danielle!" She does this right as I'm trying to drink, so naturally I spill gin and tonic all down the front of my blouse.

Adam pushes his chair back, avoiding the worst of the spill, then swoops in with a napkin, dabbing it on my shirt. When he gets most of it, he looks up, and his face is so close to mine. A smile sneaks onto his lips. "I probably should have asked before drying off your chest."

My head gives the tiniest shake, not wanting to turn away from him. "It's fine."

I see Amanda comically sneak away out of the corner of my eye, drink in hand.

"Can I ask you something?" Adam stays exactly where he is, his eyes looking deep into mine.

"Sure." My voice is barely a whisper.

"If you are no longer in a relationship, and you are not intoxicated, could we try that night at the hotel again?"

"What do you mean?"

He stands up straight, pulling away from me. "I know I said we could forget what happened, but I just can't. It took so much for me to not kiss you that night, but I didn't want to be the other guy. I wanted to be *the* guy."

I shake my head, sure I am mishearing. "What are you saying?"

"I'm shooting my shot, Danielle. If it goes badly, and you really do just want to be friends, then I have two and a half months to get over it and be happy with that. But at one point, you wanted to kiss me, and I wanted to see if that desire still existed."

"If you want to kiss me, kiss me. I put myself out there last time and got shot—"

He doesn't let me finish my idea. Instead, he swoops in, pulling me gently closer, and kisses my lips the way I deserve to be kissed.

The moment is perfect until I hear Amanda talking to the bartender. "That over there? Two of my best friends. Crazy sexual tension all year."

I start laughing against Adam's lips, then pull him in for a hug while I mouth to Amanda over his shoulder. "I can hear you."

She holds up her hands, then begins golf clapping, a smug look on her face.

I roll my eyes and look back at Adam, pulling out of our hug. "Should we try that again?"

Concern flashes across his face. "Was... was that not good?"

"No! No. It was fantastic, I just thought it might be a bit better without an audience." I gesture to Amanda, who spins away quickly as Adam looks over at her.

"Can I walk you back to school?" he asks, knowing all of my stuff is still in my classroom and that my car is still parked over there.

"Please." I get my bag and say goodbye to Amanda, who gives me the biggest hug before I go.

Adam and I walk back hand in hand, our fingers interlacing like perfectly-cut puzzle pieces. He opens the door to the building for me, and I fiddle with my classroom keys.

"Thanks for making sure I got back safely."

He gives me a smile slightly warmer than any he had given me thus far. "Anything for you."

He leans down, poised to kiss me again, and I pull away slightly, whispering, "This is a great idea," before planting my lips on his.

Chapter 22

The Year After

Forty-four books from our first kiss to our wedding, and we didn't just stick with YA. There were sci-fi and fantasy, historical fiction, and even a biography or two. We always paced our reading so we would finish at the same time, and always made sure to disagree about *something*. I loved some of the books, hated others, but always enjoyed the discussion afterward with my amazing boyfriend.

Adam is the "wait for marriage" kind of Catholic (though he never judged me for my history), so people say that's why we're getting married only a year after we started dating. In reality, I just knew what I wanted. When you're with the right person and what you both want out of life aligns so perfectly, the choice is easy. Adam knew what he saw in his future, and I found that those were the exact things I'd been longing for. And yes, I do want to get him in bed, too. If his kissing is any indication... oh boy.

I'd never had many thoughts about what I would want a wedding to look like, as I never thought it would happen for me, so when Adam asked if we could be married in the Church, I was totally down. Now here I am, across the street from where I work, about to walk down the aisle to marry my Reading Buddy, my coworker, my best friend.

Amanda is my matron of honor, of course. Her wife Bea is also attending, sitting front and center with Amanda's toddler niece who is moving in with them when I move out. All of the teachers from our school are sitting in one big group, including the new second-grade teacher who replaced Amanda. She's pretty cool, young, and nice, but no way she could take Amanda's place in my heart. Our family and friends fill out the rest of the pews.

I can only look forward, though, keeping my eyes on Adam. I can't help but think how handsome he is, all dressed up in his suit. Then he smiles and my heart melts. I don't really believe in happily ever afters, but in this moment, I can see why people do.

About the Author

Penny Pentley is a pen name of an author who is trying her hand at a new genre. She used to be an elementary teacher at a Catholic school where her favorite part of the week was Reading Buddies.

pennypentleybooks@gmail.com

Reviews help independent authors thrive. Please consider rating or reviewing this book.